DARKE
ACADEMY
SECRET LIVES

The Darke Academy series:

DARKE ACADEMY

SECRET LIVES

GABRIELLA POOLE

Hodder Children's Books

A division of Hachette Children's Books

Copyright © 2009 Hothouse Fiction Ltd

Produced by Hothouse Fiction – www.hothousefiction.com

With special thanks to Gillian Philip

First published in Great Britain in 2009
by Hodder Children's Books

The author's moral rights are hereby asserted

9

A Catalogue record for this book is available from the British Library

ISBN 978 0 340 98924 1

Typeset in Berkeley by Avon DataSet Ltd,
Bidford on Avon, Warwickshire

Printed and bound in Great Britain by
CPI Bookmarque Ltd, Croydon, Surrey

The paper and board used in this paperback by Hodder Children's Books
are natural recyclable products made from wood grown in
sustainable forests. The manufacturing processes conform to the
environmental regulations of the country of origin.

Hodder Children's Books
a division of Hachette Children's Books
338 Euston Road, London NW1 3BH
An Hachette UK company
www.hachette.co.uk

PROLOGUE

'Hey, is that you?'

She peered hopefully into the darkness, her heartbeat already quickening.

No reply. Something rustled in the undergrowth; a mosquito whined. Disappointed, she shifted her position on the old temple wall and hugged her knees. Not a footstep after all. Just some night creature. Well, he'd warned her he might be late.

Wait for me, though! Wait for me, Jess, and I'll be there . . .

She allowed herself a little grin. Of course he'd be here. They were like two magnets. He could find her instantly, in any crowd, any classroom, and he wouldn't lose her now, even in the dark. She'd scold him lightly for being late, and his laughter would make her heart turn over, just like his beautiful voice.

I love you, Jess. Don't laugh. I swear it.

No boy could fake it so well. Especially not *him*. He'd be here.

Frowning, she held up her wrist to the moonlight to peer at her watch. Ten minutes had become twenty. So what? It wouldn't feel so long in daylight. It wouldn't feel so long in a crowded noisy bar. Here in the eerie shadows of the ancient temple ruins it was easy to get spooked, that was all.

Come on.

Slipping down from the wall, she stamped her feet, rubbed her arms. Goosebumps all over them, though she wasn't cold. Another mosquito buzzed in her ear and she slapped it angrily. Gotcha.

OK, she was starting to get cross now. *A bit late* didn't mean he had any right to leave her standing here in the darkness. For thirty minutes now! This was supposed to be a romantic stroll, not a test of her nerves.

Best to let herself get mad at him, though. If she didn't get mad she could be pretty frightened, alone here in the silent shadows. Or not so silent. Her head snapped round as a dead branch cracked, as leaves rustled. That was one big rat. She shivered.

She'd liked this place in the daylight. The green lushness of jungle, gigantic roots embracing crumbling beautiful walls, warmth and life and mystery. It wasn't so great in the dark, in the shifting moon shadows that made a monster out of every massive tree, a stalking horror out of every unseen animal.

Forty-seven minutes!

Time to go. He'd had his chance and all he'd done was make a fool of her. Boy, was she going to give him an earful . . . She began to walk purposefully, then stopped. Uh-uh, she wasn't going towards the oversized rat. Shivering, swallowing hard, she took two steps back and turned.

Rustling. Creaking wood. That would be the wind.

There wasn't any wind.

Another huge rat, then, in front of her. Fine, she was going to have to go past it, but it would run as soon as it heard her coming. It was only a rat, for God's sake. Or a snake. Or . . .

Oh, just go, Jess!

She'd taken one more step when she caught the movement. That was no rat, and no snake. It was big – as big as she was. A shape moving swiftly in the hanging tangle of leaf and branch. She stepped back, and back again. It moved. Towards her. There was breathing, soft and confident and human.

'Is that you?' she called. 'Hey! Quit fooling!'

No reply.

'I mean it! Quit it!' She tried to make her voice angry, but it trembled, high-pitched. 'It's not funny.'

That sound: it might have been rotten wet leaves, stirring as a creature passed through. Or it might have been laughter, breathy and low. It couldn't be him. *Couldn't*. Anyway, there were two of them. She felt the other approaching from her right, slow, menacing. Once more she tried to shout, but when she opened her mouth all that came out was a gasp of terror.

She turned and broke into a stumbling run. It was so hard, in the darkness, keeping to the tracks. Vines and leaves slapped her face, branches tugged at her, roots snatched at her feet. Was this the path she'd taken to get here?

Path? It wasn't a path. She'd lost that, and run blindly into the trees. Her heartbeat was thunder in her ears but still she could hear them behind her, or perhaps she could only sense them. They were behind her, alongside her, herding her. What a stupid notion. But they were. *Herding her . . .*

She slithered down a low slope, scrambling over a massive root and tucking herself into the space behind. Biting hard on her knuckles, she tried not to cry. OK, she wanted to be back at home now.

Mom, this is crazy. Not real, so you can come in and

4

wake me up now. Dad, go on and laugh at me, tell me I dreamed it. Scoob . . .

Scooby. She remembered him almost bursting with pride as he waved her off to her thrilling new school: 'Bye, sis!'

'Bye, little bother! Oops – little *brother!*'

Giggling. Waving back.

Scooby . . .

Was that a sound? She breathed hard. Above her, ancient temple buildings were outlined in silver moonlight. A tree root wrapped round a pillar like the arm of a lover. Like *his* arm.

Where was he? What happened to him?

Roots, tendrils, branches: they snaked into the ancient walls, choking, hugging, strangling. Something moved in the foliage by her ear and she almost screamed, but clamped a hand over her mouth just in time. This was stupid, she thought again. Crazy. If it wasn't a dream it had to be a prank. A dumb prank.

Her body didn't think so. She was drenched in sweat: from the humidity, from running, from terror. A mosquito hummed again, and she slapped her hand against her face, suppressing a shriek. It was only an insect. Something far worse was lurking in the ruins. Hunting . . . .

Don't panic, she thought. Stay cool. There were thick entangled vines behind her, and the black maw of an ancient door, its wood long rotted away. She backed into the space, kicking frantically until the slimy leaves inside half-covered her, no longer afraid of rats or snakes or even spiders. Nothing scared her any more.

Except *them*.

She'd stay here, huddled in the ruins, until dawn broke. She'd get in trouble, she'd get laughed at, but so what? A few hours, and this place would be crawling with tourists. By then she'd probably laugh at herself. Right now those tourists were asleep in some air-conditioned hotel, dreaming of the day ahead, and of Angkor Wat, the temple of the ancients: civilisation overrun by brute nature. Wildness and beauty, sacredness and fear. So romantic and mysterious, for a tourist or a stranger.

A few hours. It wasn't so long to wait.

There were voices now in the night: distinct, hushed, but tense with the thrill of the chase. Maybe she shouldn't wait after all. Maybe she should run now. She couldn't decide. Ferociously, she rubbed her temples.

You idiot, what are you doing here anyway? You never did fit in.

A rattling flutter of wings on her cheek. She slapped at the cockroach, but only succeeded in brushing it on to her neck. It scurried down her chest and she sobbed out loud. Slamming her palm against her breastbone, she felt the bug explode into black gunge and shell fragments. She whimpered: a high-pitched noise.

The sticky roach blood made everything real. This was no dream. Out there something was hunting her down, and it was more real than school, than home, than *him*. Of course he hadn't come. Who did she think she was? Sad little, stupid little scholarship girl. He'd left her here alone and now *they* were coming . . .

Only twenty-four hours ago they'd been together, getting drunk in the streets of Phnom Penh. In love – she'd thought – and wildly excited about the flight to Siem Reap and Angkor Wat. She remembered his high laughter, both of them cheering on her beautiful, funny best friend as she struck poses and sang 'It's Raining Men' in the karaoke bar. Thrilled with her happiness, she'd turned to trace her finger across his cheekbone. Loving him . . .

She froze. A voice, clear now, close and hungry. A familiar voice, but no longer a friend's. Not singing, not flirting, not joking, but baying for her. Close. So close. And she knew it for sure. *She knew that voice.* She should run, but her blood was liquid ice in her veins.

Please. Pleasepleaseplease . . .

The voices, and a cool breath, were in her ear. 'Gotcha.'

Just for a moment, one crazy hopeful moment, she thought it was OK. Yeah, it was all a prank. A cruel joke. Hazing the girl who didn't fit in. *Oh, thank God.*

She smelled skin and sweat, tasted electric excitement and fear on the air.

'It's you,' she whispered hoarsely.

A smile, a hand reaching out to stroke her cheek. 'Not quite.'

And then she could see them clearly.

She screamed and bolted, out of the ruins, back into the jungle. She heard running feet and panting, hungry breath; saw a fast figure hurtling through the trees; smelled her own terror. And she ran.

But she knew, even then, that she could never run fast enough.

CHAPTER ONE

I *don't belong here.*

Cassie Bell came to an abrupt halt, almost tripping up the woman behind her.

'*Merde! Imbécile!*'

'Sorry!'

With a flurry of glossy shopping bags the woman stalked off, tossing another curse over her shoulder.

Cassie's temper flared. 'Waste of breath!' she yelled. 'I don't speak French!'

Either the woman didn't hear or she didn't care. Cassie felt herself shrink once more.

'Oh, hell,' she muttered. 'I *really* don't belong here.'

The buildings around her were just like that woman: tall, proud, impossibly elegant. The air was heady and rich, an elusive combination of expensive scent, late summer and exhaust fumes. Even the name of the street mocked her, since she could hardly pronounce it. What was she doing in a street with a name like that? Whatever made her think this would be a good idea? *Rue du Faubourg Saint-Honoré!* Her second-hand trainers must be an affront to the paving stones. She belonged back in Cranlake Crescent, in what they liked to call 'care'. She didn't belong in Paris.

Shoving her streaky brown hair out of her face, Cassie glanced at the scrap of paper in her hand. Considering she'd made it this far, all the way from the Gare du Nord, it'd be kind of embarrassing if she failed to find the school now. But she'd expected something in-your-face, architecturally speaking. There were some huge mansions on this street, but they were almost missable, set behind imposing walls and wrought-iron gates. The street stank of money, but not much of it was directly on show, except in the boutiques she'd passed with her jaw gaping.

Come to think of it, maybe it would be better if she couldn't find the school. It'd be a good enough excuse, because this had been a Big Mistake. OK, so she'd have to slink home to Cranlake Crescent looking like an idiot. OK, so she'd have to stomach the jeers of the other kids, the snotty told-you-so smirks from the hateful Jilly Beaton. Even worse, she'd have to face the sad disappointment in Patrick's eyes that he wouldn't quite manage to hide.

But it'd still be better than making a fool of herself like this . . .

Her heart jolted.

Cassie had barely realised she was still walking, trundling her battered suitcase behind her. She didn't know what made her glance up and across the road just at that moment. In her daze of dislocated panic she must have been on autopilot, because she was staring at a gleaming brass plaque set into a stone pillar.

The Darke Academy

Nothing else, not so much as an invitation to Please Ring the small brass bell-push set into the stone below. It all seemed very understated. Cassie could almost have been disappointed, except that even from this side of the road she could see a suggestion of the building – imposing stone pillars and pediments, the green-bronze curve of a half-hidden statue in the courtyard – behind the elaborate wrought-iron gates.

Gulping, Cassie tightened her fingers on the scabby handle of her case. She stepped off the kerb, the case bumping down on its wonky wheels behind her.

Her case.

And what was inside it? The letter that said she *did* belong here. That Cassandra Bell, of all the unlikely people, was good enough for a scholarship to the Darke Academy. The brief letter was typed on thick, expensive, parchment-like paper, and just as well – cheap paper would have fallen to bits by now, the number of times she'd unfolded and re-folded it, soaking in the words until they were acid-etched on her brain. Now it was tucked carefully inside the leatherbound notebook Patrick had given her as a leaving present, the one that must have taken a big chunk out of his council wages.

So what was she going to do? Shove the notebook back at him, and say she was sorry, she was a failure before she even arrived?

No way. That letter confirmed it. She was a student at the Darke Academy!

Grinning, Cassie ran out across the road, her case bumping behind her. A driver braked hard and yelled at her, and cheerfully she gave him the finger.

She had a right to be here. She *was* going to fit in. And what was more, she was going to *love it*.

Breathless, she let her forefinger hover over the bell-push. This is it, she thought. Here goes . . .

She retreated, startled. The gates were already swinging

wide, silent and smooth. Clenching her hand into a fist, she bit her lip. She hadn't touched the bell.

'Watch it!'

A hand on her shoulder pulled her away as a black car, long and sleek, bumped very gently across the pavement and nosed into the gates. Cassie got the impression that nothing would have halted its smooth progress, not even a careless pedestrian.

The hand let her go abruptly. As she turned, smiling, its owner backed off a step. He was a boy of about her age, tall and broad-shouldered, his brown hair close-cropped. He had the healthy look of an outdoors type, so she doubted he was usually so pale. The expression on his handsome face was one of shock; he looked as if all his blood had just drained into his scruffy trainers.

'Thanks,' she said, to break the stunned silence.

He didn't reply. Instead, turning on his heel, he walked on without another word and disappeared through the gates of the Academy. Cassie stared.

Macho, rude, and American.

It wasn't just the two drawling words that had given him away, but the downbeat clothes and his cocksure loping stride. Well, she was glad she wasn't the only one in non-deliberately-ripped jeans. Nervous again, she took a breath.

Get in there, Cassie! It's where you belong, remember?

Cassie grinned. It was like she could hear Patrick's voice right inside her head. Before the gates could swing shut again, she tugged her case through them and into the courtyard beyond.

Wow.

It was huge, far bigger than it looked from the road. Sunlight filtered through chestnut trees, dappling flagstones worn lustrous with age. The paved drive curved in a great circle round a pool that was green with ferns and exotic fleshy-leafed plants, their exposed roots trailing like twisted serpents. In the centre of the pool was the statue she'd glimpsed: a slender bronze girl on tiptoe, dreamily stretching her arms and tilting up her face to a swan. There was nothing dreamy about the swan, though. Its webbed feet clawed at the girl's body like talons, wings arched above her, its neck and savage head raised like a snake about to strike. It looked brutal and triumphant.

Cassie felt a shiver run through her. She'd always thought of swans as serene birds. Delicate. Pretty on ponds.

Not this one.

The statue was beautiful but unsettling. She turned instead to the clusters of gossiping students, voices raised with the excitement of a new term. Cassie gulped. Every single one of them was sleek with wealth and beauty. As she blew a strand of hair away from her face, she wished she'd had the cash to invest in a chic haircut. Hell, she should have *made* the cash. Mortgaged her soul to the devil or something.

When she risked a smile, they turned away, disdainful. A Japanese girl gave a bark of incredulous laughter before turning back to her friend and muttering something that made them both giggle. Like the rest of the students, they had an arrogant sheen of money and class. Of the scruffy American boy, there was no sign.

A ball of anger formed in Cassie's gut, and she tightened her grip on her case. The letter. It was in there. *Her* letter. *Her* scholarship. This crowd had bought their places here. She'd earned hers. She wasn't going to walk away from it. No way.

The black limousine was parked at the foot of a flight of stone steps and its driver was opening the rear door, black sunglasses screening his expression. Cassie watched, cynically waiting for it to disgorge another spoiled rich kid. Instead an elderly woman emerged, frail and beautiful as a withered flower.

Cassie had never imagined someone so old could be beautiful. But this woman was. Fragile, impossibly thin, like a cobweb, but still strikingly lovely. If that was what

Paris life did for you, Cassie wasn't just sticking it out, she was staying for ever.

The smile on her face died as the limousine driver closed the door with a soft clunk and slid back into the driving seat. Wasn't he even going to help the old girl up the steps? What kind of a chauffeur was he? Cassie glared at him and then at her fellow students, who weren't taking the slightest notice of the old woman.

'Unbelievable,' said Cassie loudly. Dumping her case at the foot of the steps, she went to the woman's side.

'Do you need a hand?'

Slowly, so very slowly, the old woman turned her head.

Cassie almost flinched. The woman leaned on her silver-handled stick as if it was all that was holding her up, yet there was nothing feeble about that gaze. Her eyes glittered fiercely. They weren't hostile, though. More . . . assessing.

Her skin was like crazed porcelain, translucent and webbed with lines. Perfectly white hair was swept up into a chignon. The bones of her face might have been lovingly sculpted out of granite. Cassie swallowed hard.

'I mean, if you'd rather I didn't . . . I don't want to sound . . .'

Pale lips pursed. 'Are you offering to help me, young lady?'

'Well, yes.' Cassie fidgeted, feeling a little stupid.

'How perfectly charming of you!' The imperious coolness melted into a sparkling smile. 'May I take your arm?'

Awkwardly, Cassie held it out, and gnarled fingers curled round her bicep. For an instant Cassie thought of the swan in the courtyard, its webbed feet gripping the bronze girl like talons; then she shook herself and smiled back. Behind them she heard the leopard-purr of a powerful engine, and the black car slid away.

'So lovely to have a young body,' murmured the woman.

'What?' Cassie blinked. 'I mean, I beg your pardon?'

'A young body,' she smiled, 'to help me. How kind you are.'

The grip on Cassie's arm felt surprisingly steely, but the rest of the woman was as light as a leaf skeleton. Cassie took care as she helped her up the steps. There seemed to be a lot of them.

'Thirteen steps,' mused the woman, as if reading her mind. Pausing to take a breath, she stared up at the classical façade of the school. 'It's been so long since I was last here, but I remember these steps as if it were yesterday. You're new, my dear, aren't you?'

'Is it that obvious?' Cassie grinned.

Her laugh rang like a gentle bell. 'Yes – but in the best of ways. Take my advice, ah . . . ?'

'I'm Cassandra. Everybody calls me Cassie, though.'

'Cassandra! How lovely. I shall call you Cassandra. And I am Madame Azzedine, but you will call me Estelle. And my advice is that you should take all that the Academy has to offer.'

Halting again, Madame Azzedine turned to her, fierce with excitement. 'It is the finest of schools. Indeed, the Academy is so much more than a school. Make the most of all that it can give you, Cassandra, and it will change your life. *For ever*. Do you understand me?'

'Er . . . yes.'

Madame Azzedine gave a sharp laugh. 'I think perhaps you do not. Not quite. But you will learn, my dear. You will learn so much. The Academy can change your life.'

They were only a few steps from the top now, and the old woman's breath came in rapid, shallow gasps.

'That's what I want.' Cassie almost wanted to place her hand on the one that gripped her arm. But touchy-feely wasn't in her nature, however strong her instant empathy with this kind, imperious woman. Anyway, she wouldn't put her bitten nails anywhere near that paper-skinned, immaculately manicured hand.

Madame Azzedine put the hand to her chest for a

moment, catching her breath. 'What is that, Cassandra? What do you want?'

'I want to turn my life around—'

'*Turn* it?' As they reached the top of the steps, Madame Azzedine released Cassie's arm. 'No! The Academy will teach you to conquer life, to beat it into submission and bend it to your will. True graduates of the Darke Academy take life by the throat, Cassandra! Remember that!'

A strange shiver ran down her spine, but Cassie shook it off and grinned. 'I will,' she said. 'I will!'

Smiling, Madame Azzedine clasped both Cassie's hands in hers. 'Good!'

A cough from the shadowed doorway, and Cassie almost jumped out of her skin.

'Madame, welcome.' A squat, sombre-uniformed man inclined his head. 'Sir Alric is expecting you.'

She laughed gaily. 'But of course he is! Excuse me, Cassandra, my dear. And good luck.'

'Thank you, Madame Azz— um, Estelle,' mumbled Cassie.

'And may you have many, *many* rewarding years at the Academy.' Madame Azzedine gave her a contented smile. 'I'm entirely sure you will.'

CHAPTER TWO

Cassie watched the old woman go, a little uneasy. She'd liked Madame Azzedine. Very much. It was just that . . .

Oh, for God's sake. It was just that Cassie was out of her depth. Poor old thing, she must be a hundred in the shade. How old did she think Cassie was? At fifteen, she'd have two or three years at the Academy, max, rather than many of them – assuming she didn't drop out, or get thrown out. Madame Azzedine might look fabulous for her age, but she was losing it a bit. She was no one to be afraid of. She was elegant and confident, that was all. It was time Cassie learned to be the same.

Still, Cassie thought crossly, at least she had a rough idea how to behave like a human being – unlike the staff around here. That porter, or whatever he was, didn't even offer the old girl a hand. The hatchet-faced bruiser simply tagged along as she limped into the vast, baroque hall.

Moments later they were both lost from sight.

Cassie shrugged. Nothing to do with her. Remembering that her case was still at the foot of the steps, she turned on her heel and ran back down, light-footed and even a little light-hearted.

Her heart went crashing right back into her trainers. A small group had gathered in a semicircle around her abandoned case and, as she approached nervously, the Japanese girl gave her a sidelong smirk.

'Perhaps we should call the *gendarmes*,' she announced loudly. 'I mean, it could be a bomb.'

'Oh, Keiko. I think even terrorists have a little more class.'

The speaker was an American boy, but he couldn't be more different from the guy Cassie had seen earlier. This one wore designer spectacles, leather loafers, crisp chinos and a polo shirt with a recognisably expensive logo. He looked like he'd just given his credit card a serious workout in that avenue outside.

'Now, Perry,' drawled an English boy, his hands casually in his pockets. 'Don't be uncharitable. There's such a thing as shabby chic.'

Keiko sniggered. 'Richard, how patronising. The poor are always with us, remember.'

'Now you're being unkind, Keiko,' said Perry, nudging

Cassie's case with his toe. 'The poor, after all, have a certain working class charm. This is more . . . what do the French say? Petit bourgeois?'

Richard raised an eyebrow so high it was lost in his dark floppy fringe. 'Oh, Peregrine. Now who's being petty?'

For about three seconds Cassie wanted to crawl into the nearest hole and die. The impulse passed, and the tight little burning ball of anger exploded into life. She swore, spectacularly.

'Get your hands off my stuff!' Jumping down the last few steps, she shoved Keiko aside.

Keiko looked absolutely livid, but Cassie had been in a scrap or two in her time. She clenched her fists – she could handle this stuck-up bitch. Perry the American stepped back, taking a sharp breath that sounded almost scared, but Richard only folded his arms, smiling.

'This ought to be good,' he murmured.

Cassie tensed, half-expecting Keiko to leap at her throat, but after a moment the beautiful girl laughed.

'I never touched your "stuff", scholarship girl. I wouldn't soil my hands.'

Cassie's ragged nails were digging into her palms. Oh, she'd love to punch that smirk off Keiko's face. But it was obvious that the smug little vixen wasn't going to go for anything as *bourgeois* as a fistfight. Anyway, wouldn't they just love it if she got herself expelled on her very first day?

No way. Not worth it.

'OK,' seethed Cassie. 'Now you've *proved* I'm better than you are.'

'My God,' said Perry. 'How dare you talk to Keiko like that?'

'Oh, I like it that she dares,' drawled Richard, with a lazy wink at the American boy. 'This could be entertaining! Now, Peregrine, run along. This is Few business.'

The dismissal was so peremptory that Cassie expected Perry to argue, but he backed obediently away and, with a last scowl at her, turned and jogged up the steps to the school entrance.

Richard draped a friendly arm around her shoulders. Cassie wanted to wrench it off and shove him away, but she could feel how strong he was. A wrestling match would hardly be cool, especially if she had no guarantee of winning.

'Come on, now, um . . . what's your name?'

'Cassie Bell,' she muttered.

'Well now, Cassie Bell, lighten up. We all want you to enjoy your time here. Perry and Keiko were having a little joke. Not a very funny one, I grant you,' – he got a filthy

23

look from Keiko for that – 'but you'll have to develop a thicker skin. If you want to survive, that is.'

Cassie bit back a sharp reply. The trouble was, she wasn't sure about anything. Maybe this really was how élite students behaved; how would she know? She didn't know how to behave, any more than she knew what on earth she was doing here. She didn't belong . . .

'You want to fit in, don't you?' Richard's voice was silky in her ear. 'I've got your best interests at heart, believe me—'

'Hey, *English*!'

The brash voice had an accent Cassie couldn't quite place. A second later, a girl burst on them like a tornado of energy, knocking Richard's arm away with a playful slap. She was tall, lithe as a sapling, her hair a dark, glossy tumble. Her brown eyes were fierce.

'What are you up to, English?' She wagged a slender finger in Richard's face. 'This girl, she's new, yes? Turn off that beastly charm of yours!'

'Ah, bella Isabella!' Passionately Richard seized her hand and kissed it, making Isabella's mock scowl twitch at the corners. 'I love your Latin temper as I love your flashing eyes. Yet you *so* misjudge me! Keiko and I were just acquainting young Cassie Bell with a few school rules—'

'Cassie Bell? *Cassandra?*'

Isabella turned. For an instant she looked startled, but then she smiled.

Cassie tried not to smile back. She didn't trust any of these self-assured, self-centred jerks. 'Yeah. So?'

Isabella laughed. 'So you're coming with me.' Her grip on Cassie's arm was looser than Richard's, and with her other hand she seized the handle of Cassie's case. 'Let's get you away from the riff-raff.'

With a flirtatious grin at Richard, but ignoring Keiko altogether, Isabella hauled Cassie off towards an arched colonnade at the edge of the courtyard, the case rattling and rumbling behind her.

'Hang on a minute.' Digging in her heels, Cassie jolted Isabella to a standstill. 'Don't shove me around. Who d'you think you are?'

Her aggression only made the beautiful girl hoot with laughter.

'I don't think, Cassie, I know! I'm Isabella Caruso. I'm your new roommate!'

*

'Tell me that's a print.'

Cassie came to an awestruck halt beside a massive gilt frame.

Still tugging Cassie's case along the pale-blue

carpet, Isabella turned, frowning. 'What? Oh, the Monet? No, of course it isn't a print, silly. None of them are. Do come on, Cassie.'

Tearing herself reluctantly away from the painting, Cassie followed. She was trying to look cool and uninterested and at home, but she had a terrible urge to creep along behind Isabella on tiptoe. Any minute now, someone would come along and suss her out, and then she'd be out on her ear like the fraud she was.

There's been a dreadful mistake, they'd tell her coldly. *A case of mistaken identity. You can find your way back? To Cranlake Crescent, where you belong? Naturally we will pay your fare. You look as if you need the charity . . .*

In the meantime, she might as well soak in the atmosphere. God, this was beautiful. She'd imagined such buildings existed, but only in fairytales. Didn't you need silk dresses and crinolines to hang out in a place like this? Or at least a ball of string to stop you getting lost for ever? The gilded hallways and corridors and arches seemed endless, the corniced ceilings so high she was getting a crick in her neck from staring at the gods and monsters playing in the painted sky. The soft carpet muffled even the squeaky rumble of that Saver Price suitcase.

Watching Isabella trundle it along, Cassie blushed.

Second-hand Saver Price at that, and it looked as if it might fall apart at any moment. No wonder the rich brats had laughed.

'OK, not far now. You are going to love it, Cassie— Ah!'

Isabella tugged her to a panelled door, jabbing a finger at the polished plaque set into the wood.

CASSANDRA BELL

ISABELLA CARUSO

'You see? Roommates!' Isabella could barely contain her excitement, but Cassie was struck dumb as the door swung silently open.

'You like it?' Isabella went from joyful to mournful in an instant. 'You don't like it!'

At last Cassie found her voice, but it was hoarse. 'Like it? I can't . . . There must have been a mistake.'

'No mistake.' Cheerful again, Isabella tossed Cassie's case on to one of the silk bedcovers, right next to a small mountain of designer-label luggage.

Knowing she must look as out of place as her case, Cassie felt a jab of homesickness for the cramped pit she'd shared with two other girls at Cranlake Crescent. Now, instead of compost walls and vomit-coloured skirting boards, she had rose paint and gilt, and – for God's *sake* – a chandelier. Instead of a communal bathroom that smelled of damp and toenails, she could see through a second door into an Edwardian-tiled bathroom with a claw-footed tub. Instead of squabbling over make-up and CDs with girls as foul-mouthed and hard-bitten as she was, she had a roommate who looked and acted like an exotic film star. Yet so far Isabella actually seemed . . . *nice.*

'This isn't a room, it's a palace.' Cassie didn't know whether to laugh or cry. Weak at the knees, she slumped down on the antique silk bedspread. She leaped straight back up, afraid of creasing it.

Isabella was watching her thoughtfully. 'Aha. I see the problem.'

'Oh yeah?' Cassie tensed. If this improbably beautiful girl wore even a suggestion of a mocking smirk, she'd slap it straight off her face.

'You think you are so much better than us, hey?'

Not what she'd expected. 'Hang on a minute, you—'

Isabella waved a hand airily. 'I know, I know. You have worked hard to get here, yes, yes, blah-blah. Well, Miss Hoity-Toity Scholarship Girl. You may have earned your place here, but I'll have you know that some of us have *bought* it!'

For perhaps two seconds Cassie stared open-mouthed at Isabella before she saw the girl's wide mouth twitch. In an instant she was grinning too, and then they both dissolved into laughter.

Isabella flopped back on to the soft mattress. 'You see? We are going to have fun, Cassie Bell. You and me, yes? Never mind that bore Perry Hutton, or those hoity-toity snobs from the Few. I shall teach you all about the Academy. Anyway,' she winked mischievously, 'Richard is cute and good fun, yes?'

'Yeah, sure. Whatever you say.' Cassie reached nonchalantly for her case, but she was grinning like a loon. She'd never made a friend quite so instantly. Actually she'd barely made any friends at all, she thought ruefully. 'And in return, I'll teach you some proper English. Nobody says "hoity-toity" any more, OK?'

'No?'

'We say, "Keiko's really up herself".'

'Up herself. Right!' Isabella giggled.

'So who are the Few? Are they sort of prefects or something?'

'Something like that. Let's not talk about them just now. No! Don't unpack. Come on.' Isabella grabbed her hand. 'We are going to explore!'

*

'Tell me about the scholarship! Come on, scholarship girl!'

29

Cassie gave Isabella a sidelong smile. Scholarship girl. The more Isabella used the term in an affectionate way, the less it would sting when someone like Keiko used it as a jibe – and Cassie had a feeling her roommate knew that.

'Nothing to tell. There was kind of an exam, but it wasn't that hard.'

'I bet it was,' said Isabella solemnly. 'I bet I could not do it. I came to the Academy because my father is very rich. In here?' She tapped her temple. 'I'm as thick as a log.'

'As a *plank*,' said Cassie dryly, 'and you are not. Anyway, there was an interview too. They wanted to know everything. What I'd studied, what I thought, where I came from. Like they were picking my brains. Just as well Patrick coached me.'

'And he is . . . ?'

'Don't give me that!' Cassie laughed. 'He's my key worker at the home, OK? He's lovely. Pity he isn't the manager.' She gave an angry shiver as she remembered that night last month. Waking in the night as usual, she'd overheard the familiar, whip-like voice cutting into the new girl, a skinny, sullen, tear-stained eleven-year-old. *Self-harming, is it now, miss? What won't you do for a bit of attention? I'd cut a bit deeper if I were you.* 'Jilly Beaton's a vicious cow. Inspectors love her, but she's a cow when they've gone.'

'Back home in Argentina,' sniffed Isabella, 'cows are very important, but they know their place.'

The horrible memory dissipated on the spot. Stifling a laugh, Cassie elbowed Isabella in the ribs. 'Anyway, Patrick's great. I dunno what I'd have done without him. He kept badgering me to go for the scholarship. Said somebody else he knew had won a place and I could do it too, if I tried. And know what? He was right.'

'But of course he was. Now, I think we've seen everything except the gardens. And the sixth-form building, of course, but that is separate, on the other side of the street. Meanwhile, here we are! Back at the main entrance hall.'

Really? Cassie must have lost her bearings. She had been in this soaring space before, of course, but only just, peering in to watch Madame Azzedine disappear into the shadows. Now she had to gasp.

A great curving staircase swept down from where they stood to a marble-tiled hallway. The stairs were supported by massive pillars, and between each pillar was a white statue on a plinth. Gods and monsters again, gleaming like alabaster. The gilding was lavish enough to take

Cassie's breath away, and even Isabella was starry-eyed with pride.

'Isn't it beautiful, Cassie? I hope we will stay here longer than a term. It is one of the most beautiful venues we have had. Well, in my time. I think the school has been here before, but a very long time ago.'

'What d'you mean? It hasn't always been here?'

With a peal of laughter, Isabella linked her arm through Cassie's. 'We have only just come here! The Academy moves every term, you didn't know?'

'No. Every *term*? Seriously?'

'Every term. Last term we were in Sydney! *So* exciting. Spring term, Moscow. And last year at this time it was Rio de Janeiro! I *loved* Rio.'

Cassie gaped. 'It moves all over the world?'

'But of course! With the Academy I have studied in Cape Town, in Bangkok, in Madrid . . . Oh, I can barely remember.' Isabella tossed her hair. 'It is what makes it so exciting to be a student here. They did not tell you this?'

'No, they never said. But I mean, why move?' Cassie was surprised at the stab of disappointment. 'It's so beautiful here.'

'Everywhere the Academy goes is beautiful,' said Isabella dismissively. 'Sir Alric would not have it any other way. Ah! *Jake!* Jake Johnson! Don't you dare pretend you haven't seen me!'

At the foot of the stairs a boy turned from a blonde girl and looked up. Close-cropped brown hair and beaten-up jeans: Cassie recognised him straight away. The American – the macho one with the bad manners. He grinned up at Isabella as she ran down the stairs two at a time, then glanced at Cassie, raising a hand in hesitant greeting. There was no time for more. Isabella threw herself into his arms and gave him a smacking kiss on each cheek.

Which was brave, thought Cassie, considering how Jake's companion was glaring at her.

If Jake was good-looking, the blonde girl was stunning. Her eyes were icy-blue and her face was rigid with disdain, but she was still beautiful. Like the Snow Queen, thought Cassie, remembering old picture books. The diamonds sparkling in her ears weren't as hard and cold as she was, but boy, was she lovely. Her skin was just radiant. Like winter sun.

'Jake!' whooped Isabella, detaching herself.

'It's great to see you, Isabella,' he said, with a sidelong glance at the blonde goddess.

There was something formal and withdrawn in his tone, and Isabella's face clouded with disappointment.

Her smile grew a little nervous as she turned to the blonde. 'Hello, Katerina.'

'Hello, Isabella.'

The voice was throaty, the accent clipped. Scandinavian? wondered Cassie. German? She was reminded of old movies on boring Saturday afternoons in Cranlake Crescent. Katerina was ethereal and distant, like Greta Garbo, maybe, or Ingrid Bergman. Cool as a Hitchcock blonde.

'Isn't it wonderful to be back, darling? And who is this?' Her intent smile made Cassie fidget. 'Were we permitted to bring personal staff this term? I wish they had told me.'

Blood rushed to Isabella's face. 'No, Katerina, this is—'

Managing to contain her irritation – just – Cassie made herself hold out her hand. 'I'm Cassie Bell. I'm the new scholarship girl.'

Isabella sagged with relief. Katerina put her fingers to her mouth.

'Oh, do forgive me.' Gracefully she took Cassie's extended hand. 'Always, always I am so clumsy. Am I not, Jake?' Her smile sparkled.

'No way, Katerina!'

'That's kind of you, Jake. Cassie, welcome to the Academy. I'm sure it will be a *completely* new experience for you, and that you will learn very much.'

34

With a superhuman effort, Cassie kept smiling. She wished Katerina would wipe her own off her face. The girl was all teeth.

'Well. So much to do. The Few have called a Congress for tomorrow, and I must help with the preparations.' She gave Isabella a glance that to Cassie seemed sly and taunting.

Oh, for crying out loud, thought Cassie. Her imagination was working in overdrive. Katerina had smiled at Isabella, that was all. The girl had the tact and sensitivity of a Rottweiler, but she wasn't Cruella de Vil. If Cassie didn't stop making these snap judgements, she was never going to make any friends.

'Bye, Katerina,' she managed. 'Nice to meet you.'

'Likewise, I'm sure. Goodbye, Jake.' Katerina let her hand linger on his arm. 'I'll see you later.' With a last smile, she stalked off, graceful as a panther.

Isabella had fallen silent. Jake's cheekbones reddened as he stared after Katerina with yearning. Cassie cleared her throat and swallowed her pride.

'Thanks,' she said brightly. 'You saved me from a messy death this morning.'

'Oh?'

'Under a car? At the gate?'

'Oh. Yeah.' Jake scratched his neck awkwardly.

'That's OK. I'm sorry I was kinda curt. You gave me a . . . a fright.'

'Well. They wouldn't really have run me over, of course.'

'You reckon?' he said darkly, before abruptly changing the subject. 'So you're enjoying Fresh Meat Day?'

Cassie made a face. 'I beg your pardon?'

'Jake!' scolded Isabella.

'I'm sorry, did I say Fresh Meat? I meant Freshman Day, of course.' Cassie blinked at his bitter sarcasm. 'Listen, Isabella, it's great to see you, but I need to go register for classes. See you later, 'kay?'

'Oh. OK.' Her disappointment was way too obvious.

'Nice to meet you, then,' said Cassie.

'And you,' said Jake abruptly. 'Welcome to the Academy. Oh, Isabella?'

'Yes, Jake?'

For heaven's sake, thought Cassie. The girl might as well have *Ask anything of me* tattooed on her forehead.

Jake nodded at Cassie, but he was looking at Isabella. 'Take care of her, OK? You know this place. She doesn't.'

'Sure, Jake. You know I will.'

'Patronising git,' muttered Cassie as he strode away.

Isabella tore her gaze away from his retreating back to

stare at Cassie. 'No, really, he's just a bit . . .'

Cassie gave her a slow grin.

Isabella shrugged, bit her lip ruefully. 'Just a bit up himself?'

'You got it.'

They both laughed, Isabella a little too hysterically.

Isabella linked her arm through Cassie's. 'Let's go and register.'

'All right. I—'

Something prickled the back of Cassie's neck. Frowning, she turned.

At the curve of the stairs stood a boy, immaculately dressed in a stylish black suit. A book was open in his hand, but he wasn't reading it; he was watching her, intently, and he seemed to be holding his breath. She expected him to be embarrassed, but he didn't turn away. His dark, pellucid stare was riveted on hers, but he didn't smile.

Cassie didn't either. Her neck tingled again. She felt a sort of thrilling surprise at his nerve, but if he wasn't going to look away, why should she? He was black-haired, tawny-skinned, and beautiful. As beautiful as Katerina, but in a different way. His beauty wasn't cold. It was serious and warm and the word *noble* popped into her head—

For God's sake! What was she thinking? She tugged at Isabella's arm.

'Come on!' she hissed.

'It's OK.' There was laughter in Isabella's voice. 'You can look, you know. You might as well. That is all anyone gets to do with *him*.'

'Why?' She would not, would not, *would not* turn back to see if he was still there. Even though the effort was killing her.

'That,' said Isabella, 'is Ranjit Singh.'

CHAPTER THREE

Cassie kicked off the last cotton sheet and lay spreadeagled, staring up mesmerised at the chandelier. It winked in the moonlight, tinkling gently. Half an hour ago she'd pulled the heavy damask curtains a little apart and slid the window open, but it hadn't helped. The room was too hot, the bed way too soft. Her cheap supermarket pyjama T-shirt clung to her skin. And Isabella, sleeping the comatose sleep of the innocent, was snoring gently.

Cassie gave her roommate a wry grin. Nice that even tempestuous Latin American beauties snored. Anyway, Cassie had no intention of waking her. Of course Isabella wasn't going to be as over-excited as a scholarship girl on her first night.

Oh, this was hopeless. Sliding off the bed, she padded back to the window and pulled the curtain a little wider.

Recognisable landmarks sparkled like huge jewels, familiar from the books Patrick had shown her: the Arc de Triomphe, the towering obelisk in the place de la Concorde, the Eiffel Tower. Earlier tonight, Isabella had hauled her across to the window.

'It's so beautiful, look! *La ville lumière*, Cassie – the City of Light!' Isabella had laughed with delight. 'What better place for the Darke Academy?'

Their room was three floors up. How much more, Cassie wondered, would she see from the top?

In the oppressive heat Cassie couldn't bear to pull on her dressing gown and slippers. Anyway, her T-shirt-and-baggies ensemble was perfectly decent, if a bit lacking in the Parisian style department. As she eased open the door, Isabella stirred, turned over, and resumed her snoring. Exhaling, Cassie slipped out into the corridor.

She was relieved to see that small wall lamps burned softly, creating pools of light in the darkness. Not that she was afraid of the dark. She knew there were worse things to be afraid of than ghosts and vampires and werewolves.

Words, for instance. Words were like fangs, if they were sharpened by an expert like Jilly Beaton. Words could bite deep.

Oh, you're a worthless little slut, Cassandra Bell. Even a worthless big slut like your mother didn't want you.

She used to be scared of Jilly Beaton. Too scared to tell anyone about her vile bullying.

No one will believe you, anyway, filthy little liar that you are! It's in your file – compulsive liar. You try telling anyone and I'll have your privileges withdrawn again.

So Cassie never had told anyone. She learned to fend for herself instead. And as she got older and taller, and discovered that a cold, blank gaze of hatred worked better than crying or shouting, Jilly Beaton left her alone and picked on smaller kids instead. Only now Jilly never knew when she would turn away from tormenting some poor girl to find Cassie watching silently, her eyes full of the silent promise of retribution, one day. That seemed to put her off. Made her keep her distance and bought the other girls some relief, if only for a few weeks.

Cassie shivered, wishing she'd worn her dressing gown after all. At least she'd had Patrick. She trusted him – just not with everything, that was all. He'd brought her out of herself, made her laugh, taught her she *wasn't* worthless. And now here she was, at one of the most prestigious schools in the world.

Life was funny . . .

Barefoot, she crept towards the grand staircase. She

wasn't scared, but boy, this place was creepy. If she thought too much, if she listened too hard, she could almost hear sounds. Creaks. Whispers. The sigh of a faint breeze. A footfall.

Oh, don't be daft. She gave herself a mental slap.

No. There it was again. Freezing, she strained to listen.

Yes. Definitely. The sound came from below. A very soft step; if it hadn't fallen on the marble floor of the entrance hall, she'd never have heard it. This wasn't the careful tread of someone who didn't want to disturb sleepers – it was someone who didn't want to be discovered. Cassie knew the difference.

An intruder? Hesitantly, she put a hand on the gilded banister and peered down into the gloom.

Moonlight and shadows, and for an instant the hall was full of ghosts. Her heart turned over in her chest, but a second later Cassie recognised the white shapes. The statues she'd seen earlier.

Something was still wrong, though. Achilles was slaying Hector, mercilessly, but there were only two marble figures on that plinth. So why were three shadows cast on to the floor?

Someone was hiding. Whoever it was had ducked behind the plinth when they heard someone coming. Now Cassie could also hear unmuffled footsteps. As she watched, holding her breath, the squat porter appeared and stood still, silently alert.

Cassie didn't dare breathe, and she didn't dare move back in case the movement drew his attention. She could only hope he wouldn't look up. She couldn't say why, but she knew, instinctively and for certain, that she didn't want that dead-eyed, brutish porter to catch her out of her room. She wouldn't want him to catch anyone. Not even a burglar.

At last he turned, clearly unwilling to investigate every shadow in the hallway, and his footsteps faded.

Beneath Hector's dying body, the third shadow moved, slipping from the shelter of the statue and heading for the grand staircase. Her heart in her throat, Cassie backed away, hunting frantically for a place to hide. The prowler was going to come up the grand staircase – right past her. *Damn.* She went cold with fear. There were no convenient curtains, only shadows and a small alcove. She pressed herself back, staying absolutely still.

His footfalls were almost silent now on the rich carpet, but when she sensed him coming she took a small breath and held it, making no sound. Except for her heart, of course, thrashing like a triphammer, but luckily he couldn't hear that. Nor did he see her, as he passed close by like a phantom.

Jake Johnson.

She frowned. What was he up to? For a moment she longed to go back to her room. Her nice, safe, beautiful room with her softly snoring roommate. She could put up with a little insomnia.

Only one thing wrong with that scenario, decided Cassie: she didn't like night skulkers. They were never up to any good. If something was wrong, she wanted to be first to know. Knowledge was power: she'd learned that lesson well at Cranlake Crescent.

Anyway, what was there to be afraid of? Waiting until Jake had turned on to the next landing, she slipped from the shadows and followed.

Damn, he was good. His antennae were a lot better than Jilly Beaton's. He knew to pause unexpectedly, to listen for someone following. He could move swiftly and use the darkness just like she did. At the top of the stairs, she almost lost the trail.

He had slipped into an upper corridor. The blackness was more complete here on the deserted topmost floor: the ceiling was low and the only light leaked up from the lower levels. Cassie's curiosity was strong enough to beat her nerves, though. She stepped into the corridor.

As her eyes adjusted, she made out an arched smear of light. Curling her bare toes into the soft, comforting carpet, she took another trembling step, then another. OK: now she was committed. *Go, Cassie! What are you scared of?*

Her progress was painfully slow. She half-expected Jake to leap out, but he was nowhere to be seen. Then, after far too long, she made out his silhouette ahead. About to hurry after him, she came to a dead halt.

That couldn't be *another* set of footsteps? Surely they had to be Jake's.

No. These steps were behind her. Less guarded, but still furtive. And definitely on the grand staircase. The sinister porter? Maybe. What would he do if he thought she'd been sneaking around? Shop her to the teachers? Or deal with her himself? And what if it *wasn't* the porter . . .

Oh, God.

Cassie broke into an uncertain run. Just as panic began to swamp her, she saw the arch of light grow larger, and then she was beneath it. Grabbing the plasterwork, she leaned back, trying to get her terrified breathing under control. Once more she heard a footfall, and made her decision. She swung round the corner and into a smaller stairway.

It was like bright day after the terrible darkness of the corridor. She wasn't even worried about alerting Jake any more; somehow that wouldn't be as bad as being caught by whoever – or whatever – was behind her. Jake was a fast-moving blur, slipping round the stairs two floors down, but she was almost desperate to catch up with him now, whatever the consequences. Grabbing the banister, she went silently down.

Reaching the third floor, Jake turned through an archway. Swallowing her fear, Cassie waited a moment. The footsteps behind her still echoed softly. Not much time. Setting her jaw, she peered cautiously round the corner.

The new passageway was maybe thirty feet long. It was well, if eerily, lit by rows of small alcoves, each one occupied by a classical bust. Jake must have a colossal nerve, thought Cassie. The guard of marble heads looked scarily real, their blank eyeballs terrifying. Yet Jake must have passed between them, because he was crouching at a door at the end of the corridor, testing the handle.

It wasn't giving way to him. He worked something into the lock, pushing and twisting frantically, but when he tried the handle again it still didn't give. He glanced fearfully up into the recesses on either side of the door, but nothing moved, no one challenged him. After a few more tries at the lock, he leaned against the door, pressing his head to the wood like someone in despair.

Uh-oh. He was about to give up, and if he turned now he'd see her for sure. Time to go. Taking three quick steps backward, she hesitated.

No way was she retreating upstairs to that pitch-black corridor, towards that second set of echoing footsteps. No. She'd go down instead, and try to find her way back another way. She plunged down the stairs, breaking into a half-run. If she could just get to the bottom, she'd be safe, she was sure. Almost there . . .

Cassie was halfway down the last flight when she felt an icy chill settle between her shoulder blades. She was being watched.

Halting abruptly, she sank her teeth into her lower lip and tried not to scream. It was too late to try to hide. If she turned she'd see whoever, or whatever, was behind her – and she really, *really* didn't want to. Maybe it was the porter. Maybe it was Jake. But who knew what else might be lurking in this eerie place in the small hours?

Stupid. What a coward she was. Of course she had to look! Gritting her teeth, Cassie spun and scowled up.

The watching eyes glowed. Cassie went rigid with fear.

Unhurried, the figure drew back.

A tremor shuddered down her spine. Not Jake. Not the porter. Yet there was something about that silhouette – something about its stillness – that was alarmingly familiar. She'd felt that cool, animal gaze before, tingling on the nape of her neck.

She had no way of proving it, even to herself, but Cassie knew it in her bone marrow.

You might as well look, Cassie! That's all anyone gets to do with him . . .

CHAPTER FOUR

'Maths!' moaned Isabella. 'Why must we begin with maths?'

Clutching her textbooks under one arm, Cassie squeezed her roommate's elbow consolingly. 'We have to start with something. It's not so bad.'

'It's a terrible omen. I shall fail this year, I know I shall. Papa will be furious.'

'You mean he'll refuse to buy you a new string of polo ponies?' Jake Johnson fell into step beside them. 'You poor heiress. Just make do with the old ones.'

Isabella elbowed him, not gently. 'Be kind to me, Jake. I am too fragile to withstand your scorn.' She tossed her mane of hair. 'A delicate southern flower.'

Jake laughed out loud. 'Yeah, and shall I show you the rib you just broke?'

'Any time.' She gave him a sweet smile.

Cassie was amused but anxious. Isabella's flirting seemed a lot more serious than Jake's. Anyway, wasn't he stuck on Frosty the Snow Woman? She didn't want her roommate to go falling in unrequited love.

Besides, what was he up to?

Jake looked cheerful, uncomplicated, *American*. He seemed like a normal guy. It was hard to believe she'd trailed him last night. Cassie could almost have believed that she'd dreamed it – if it hadn't been for the shadows of tiredness under his brown eyes. When he smiled at her, she didn't smile back, and he frowned slightly.

I don't know what you're up to, but I know you're up to something . . .

Uneasy, Jake returned all his attention to Isabella. 'Anyway, Miss Caruso, mathematics is just what you need. The highest achievement of reason.' A broad grin softened his chiselled face. 'It does not yield to violent emotion. It brings order out of complete chaos. Am I getting through? *Ow!*'

She slapped him again with a textbook. 'If you are going to insult me, Jake Johnson, I will not speak to you for the whole term. Ah!' Isabella's face brightened as she pulled Cassie to a halt beside a huge portrait. 'This you must see, Cassie. You, Jake Johnson – go away.'

'Hey!' He held up both hands, still grinning. 'I consider

my ass whupped. Anyway,' he jerked a thumb at the painting, 'you'll excuse me if I don't stay to genuflect.' He sauntered towards the classroom.

Isabella was scowling. 'That boy is impossible!' she exclaimed. 'No respect. For *anyone*. Not even for this amazing man.' She flourished her fingers at the painting. 'Look, Cassie. This may be all you ever see of him.'

'Yeah?' The portrait was so big Cassie had to take a step back to see it properly. 'Who is it?'

'*This* is Sir Alric Darke.'

Cassie studied him. So this was the legendary founder of the Darke Academy? The portrait was a modern one, his angular face defined in deceptively casual brushstrokes. His eyes burned with vivid intelligence, their colours melding into grey but glinting like mica in granite. His silver-streaked dark hair grew in a perfect widow's peak, one stray strand of it curving down his forehead like a thin blade. He had been painted at his desk, a book open beneath his hand, and he was watching the artist with an expression of cold, probing curiosity. Cassie felt he was looking straight into her brain and soul.

'Jeez,' she said after a moment. 'I bet those eyes follow you around the room.'

'Striking, don't you think?' Isabella tugged her arm.

'Come on, Cassie, you cannot stand here for ever. We'll be late!'

Cassie let Isabella pull her towards the classroom, but she couldn't help turning back once. Yup, they did follow you.

'Miss Caruso.' The maths teacher peered over his half-moon specs as Isabella flounced into the room. 'It's the first day of term. Please don't tell me your time-keeping is going to be as execrable as your algebra. Again.'

'Oh, Herr Stolz, I am so sorry.' Isabella threw him a lovely smile as she tugged Cassie towards two empty desks. 'I just know you will make something of me this term.'

Someone at the back of the class murmured a few words that Cassie didn't catch. She glanced round: Katerina. The girl at her side spluttered with laughter.

Keiko. Of course.

Taking no notice, Isabella dumped her books on her desk.

Stolz forced his twitching mouth into a scowl. 'Leading astray our new girl, too? Shame on you, Isabella. But welcome to the Academy, Cassie. I saw your test paper – very impressive. I'm expecting great things from you.'

Cassie felt blood rush to her face as every student

turned to stare at her. She slid into her chair, shoulders hunched, trying to occupy the tiniest amount of space possible. When Isabella gave her a dig in the ribs, though, she gasped and sat upright, shoulders jerking back. Jake wasn't kidding about the broken rib.

As Stolz turned to scribble on the blackboard, Jake himself leaned across from the desk on her left. 'It's all the polo,' he explained in a stage whisper. 'She's deadly with a mallet. So I'm told.'

'Ignore him,' hissed Isabella. 'Now, Cassie. The cute blond boy, that is Dieter. He is from Bavaria. Cormac – beside him – he is from Dublin. Doesn't he have beautiful blue eyes?' Blatantly, Isabella pointed out more students. 'Ayeesha is from the West Indies. Barbados, I think. She is very nice –' she lowered her voice, 'much nicer than some of *them*.' Disparagingly, she nodded in the direction of Keiko and the group at the back of the room, before resuming her introductions. 'That is Ayeesha's roommate next to her. Her name is Freya: Norwegian. Alice: she is English, like you. Perry Hutton you know, worse luck, and poor Richard has to share with him.' She sniffed. 'Jake's roommate is South African: Pumzile, there. He has a twin, Graca, but she is in the other Year Eleven class. It's just as well they split those two up, if you ask me—'

'*MISS CARUSO!*'

'Sorry.' She smiled sweetly.

'No, you're not,' muttered Jake.

'And you, Mr Johnson,' said the teacher, who hadn't turned round, 'if you'd be good enough to give me your attention instead of flirting, perhaps you could let me know what x would equal in this equation?'

'Sure,' said Jake. He didn't even look at the board. 'It's b minus y divided by z, am I right? No, 's OK, Herr Stolz. I know I'm right.'

'Too clever for your own good, Jake.' But Stolz was smiling.

'You can say that again,' drawled someone from the back of the class.

Cassie turned. Yes, she'd recognised the voice: Richard, the smooth English boy, gave her a warm smile and a flirtatious wink. He and Keiko and Katerina sat together in that 'not-so-nice group' Isabella had pointed out. What struck Cassie, now she had a chance to stare at them, was their sheer collective beauty. They looked like an advertising pull-out in some glossy magazine: *Vanity Fair*, maybe, or *Vogue*, one of those posh monthlies Jilly Beaton used to read.

Katerina sat alert, her Mont Blanc fountain pen tapping prettily against her chin. Keiko, on the other hand, was adjusting her lipstick in a small mirror, one enamelled fingernail flicking at the corner of her mouth. Richard's long legs were stretched out before him, his hands linked behind his head. He couldn't have looked more uninterested in equations if he'd tried.

Cassie waited for Stolz to snap at Richard as he'd snapped at Isabella and Jake, but he didn't. He didn't even turn round. As he stared fixedly at the blackboard, his neck reddened, and he rubbed it anxiously with one hand, getting chalk in his hair.

'Mr Halton-Jones.' He paused again. 'I hardly think—'

'Oh, come, come, Herr Stolz.' Richard yawned and stretched. 'Our American friend is showing off. Challenging your authority, I'd say. Not a good start to the term for him. Or you.'

'Richard!' hissed Ayeesha, turning in her chair to scowl at him. 'That's enough.'

Jake bristled.

Stolz's voice was conciliatory. 'Mr Halton-Jones, believe me, I don't mind when I get such accurate and quick answers. Now—'

'In fact, I think that exact equation is an example in the new textbook.' Richard frowned, pursing his lips. 'I'm sure I saw it.'

'The hell it is,' snapped Jake.

'Well, Jake, if you feel the need to cram during the holidays so you can keep up with the rest of us, that's nothing to be ashamed of.'

Jake half-rose. 'You can kiss my—'

'Gentlemen!' barked Stolz. The red flush had crept up to his cheekbones. 'Jake, sit down. I will not have such behaviour in my classroom. See me afterwards.'

Cassie exchanged a shocked glance with Isabella, who raised her eyebrows. Stolz simply turned back to the board, consulting the book in his left hand. It trembled very slightly.

'Richard.' A languid voice broke the awkward silence. 'Ayeesha is quite right. Behave yourself. You are setting our new scholarship girl a bad example.'

Richard grinned. 'Whatever you say, Katerina. I do apologise.'

'In fact, we must all apologise.' Katerina checked her watch. 'Herr Stolz, a Congress has been called for the Few. Please do excuse us?' Her expectant smile was sweet, but she was already gathering her books. So were several other students.

Only Ayeesha looked embarrassed as she got to her feet. 'I'm so sorry, Herr Stolz. You should have been notified.'

Stolz turned. 'Thank you, Ayeesha. You're right,

I wasn't informed, but – yes, of course.' He tightened his fingers on the chalk, and it snapped. 'You may go.'

Waste of breath, thought Cassie. They were already going, and Stolz wasn't even trying to delay them. The expression on his face was a weird mixture of fury, apprehension and relief.

'Incidentally, Ranjit sends his apologies.' Katerina's tongue lingered on the name. Her attention flicked around the rest of the class, then came to rest on Stolz. 'He had important Few business this morning, but hopes to resume his classes tomorrow.'

Cassie couldn't help but gasp. Nobody else took any notice as the students left the room, all chatting easily except for the silently apologetic Ayeesha. Keiko threw one last scowl in Cassie's direction, and then they were gone.

The rest of the class waited expectantly as Stolz fiddled with the broken chalk. Cassie couldn't believe what she was seeing. That crowd might have asked the teacher's permission to leave, but they hadn't waited for the answer. And who did Ranjit Singh think he was?

Stolz made no comment, no comment at all.

'Now.' He cleared his throat and jabbed his stub of chalk viciously at the board. 'The value of z . . .'

*

'What was *that* about?' Cassie liked maths, but she'd been itching for the lesson to end so she could buttonhole Isabella in the corridor. 'Are classes optional for prefects, or what?'

Isabella pushed her hair carelessly behind her ear. 'They're not prefects. They're the Few. They do more or less as they like.' Shrugging, she marched down the corridor. 'Some of them take advantage, some of them don't.'

'But who *are* they?'

'The Few – I told you. Sir Alric's favourites.' She flicked her fingers dismissively.

'But they don't seem to give a toss about the teachers.'

'Well. They are *much* more important than mere teachers, Cassie.'

'Oh, come on.'

'Seriously. The Few practically run the school. Not officially, of course, but that's how it really is. Don't get on the wrong side of them, is my advice to you. Some of them are perfectly nice, but others . . .'

'That's crazy. Who gets to be, er, Few?'

Isabella shrugged, snorting. 'The best and cleverest and most beautiful. Hah!'

Cassie nudged her, grinning. 'So why aren't you one of them?'

Isabella laughed. 'You're too kind, Cassie. You want me to tell you the truth? They have not asked me! There.'

'That's kind of hard to believe,' said Cassie. 'Maybe the mean ones are jealous. Blackballing you or something. You're much better looking than Keiko, and I bet you're smarter too.'

'Oh, sure. And she knows it.' Isabella grinned at her. 'Well, they have an initiation this term, that's what I hear. That means someone else joins the Few.'

'Then it has to be you!'

'They can ask, if they like. Or not. As they wish.' Isabella tilted her chin haughtily. 'Perry Hutton is – what do you say? – gagging for it. But it's not as if I care one way or the other.'

Yeah, thought Cassie dryly. Sure.

'What about Katerina? Is she Head Girl?'

'Boss Cat, more like.' Isabella wrinkled her nose.

'Where's she from?'

'Sweden,' said Isabella carelessly.

Oh, right. So Cassie's movie-star casting had been spot-on. Not that she could imagine Katerina ever Vanting to Be Alone, though. Who else was Swedish? Abba? Cassie wrinkled her nose. Not such a good comparison.

'I can see her in a silver catsuit, though,' she muttered under her breath.

'What? Oh, look. Here they come.' Isabella dug her in the ribs.

The chattering throng of students in the marble hall quietened, parting nervously. Through them came the missing students from their maths class, together with another six or seven others, equally beautiful. Some of them – Ayeesha, a blonde girl at her side, and the Irish boy, Cormac – called to friends and peeled off from the haughty group. The others stalked past their fellow students as if no one existed but themselves.

'They must have finished their Congress. You see? Sir Alric's favourites cannot even have meetings like anyone else. They have to have a *Congress*.'

Cassie got the impression Isabella wanted to spit, but her air of mischief was quickly restored. 'Cassie, come! I must introduce you to Ranjit!'

Oh, God.

Why the bolt of sheer terror? Cassie shook her head. He was only a *boy*. Kind of a beautiful one, though, and even nicer up close. Fanciable. And he had style too. His black jacket was as sharp as anything she'd seen, but he wore it with a casual confidence that Cassie had never seen in someone of her own age. She felt her mind drain of all intelligent thought as Isabella dragged her up to him.

'Ranjit!'

He turned, and Cassie took a breath. He was standing right beneath one of the more stunning statues. God, thought Cassie, he makes Achilles look like a slob . . .

It was hard to believe those gentle amber eyes had seemed so frightening last night.

Ranjit nodded. 'Isabella.'

The Argentinian girl kissed him briskly. Cassie hoped she wasn't going to cut herself on his cheekbones. 'Ranjit, this is Cassie Bell. She is new here. Say hello!'

'Hello,' he said, 'Cassandra Bell.'

She managed to smile. Or something. More of a grimace, really. She'd never heard such a low and beautiful voice, and it made her insides mush. God Almighty. The only word that popped into her head – apart from *wow* – was *unattainable*.

'Cassandra Bell,' he repeated. 'You're the—'

'Scholarship girl,' she said tightly.

Ranjit made an odd face that was half-smile, half-frown. 'I was going to say, you're the clever one.'

'Oh,' said Cassie lamely. 'Right.'

'So, what do you think of the place so far?'

Blimey. He sounded genuinely interested. Perhaps not so unattainable after all.

'Well, it's very different—' she began, but Ranjit's gaze was already slipping past her.

'I'm sure,' he interrupted brusquely, his focus now somewhere over her left shoulder. 'Well, excuse me.' And with that he turned away and vanished into the crowd.

Ouch. Cassie had never felt so comprehensively snubbed. Not so interested, then.

'Oh.' Coming to a halt beside them, Katerina pouted. 'Always rushing off. Poor Ranjit. *So* hard-working.'

Richard was at Katerina's shoulder, and he murmured in her ear, 'Didn't you have something to discuss with him?'

'I did indeed.' Smiling, Katerina kissed him on the cheek and slipped away.

Now she'd had a moment to recover, Cassie's empty feeling of shock was rapidly being filled up with anger. Poor Ranjit, indeed. Who did the stuck-up tosser think he was?

If anyone in this place deserved sympathy, it was Jake. Just about every boy in the hall was surreptitiously ogling Katerina, but the American, belatedly arriving after his scolding from Stolz, was hypnotised. Even when the Swede had disappeared from sight, he still stared after her. Oh, he had it bad all right. But the boy wearing his heart on his sleeve this morning was the same boy who was prowling the corridors last night. What was he up to?

'Cassie Bell, you're quite the star.'

Cassie jumped back into reality as Richard took hold of her arms and kissed her cheek before she had time to jerk away.

She gave him a suspicious look. 'Oh, yeah?'

'Stolz's new golden girl – the maths genius. You'll put me to shame.'

'Really?' she said coolly. 'I thought the rest of us had to *cram* to keep up with you.'

'*Touché!*' He winked. 'Not the rest of you. Just the one.' He leaned closer to whisper in her ear. 'Actually, me and Jake? It's pure jealousy on my part. Those hawkish eyes, that grim jaw, the shaved hair. He's so all-American, they could carve him on Mount Rushmore, couldn't they?' Releasing her, he sighed, folding his arms. 'And that grungy chic! The foppish looks of an Englishman cannot compare.'

Cassie found herself returning his mischievous grin. Well, at least he was honest. Cutely self-deprecating, too. It was an appealing combination, especially coming from a boy who looked as much like a young god as the rest of the Few.

'Oh, you're not that ugly,' she told him airily.

Seizing her hands, he brought them to his lips and kissed them, then pressed them to his heart. She could feel his heartbeat through white cotton. Taken aback, she threw a *help me!* look at Isabella, but the Argentinian didn't do anything of the sort. Her expression was delighted, and kind of smug. Cassie tried to glower at her, but couldn't quite manage it.

'You've made my day.' Richard's smile was high-wattage. 'Let me buy you a coffee and show you a little of Paris. I know this *perfect* little café in the Marais. Nine o'clock tomorrow?'

'Don't we have lessons?'

'It's a study morning. Time off to look at the city. Immerse ourselves in its culture. Where shall we meet? Right here? You are my angel, Cassie Bell.' He blew her a kiss, then disappeared in Katerina's wake.

Cassie blinked. 'How the hell did that happen?'

Isabella laughed. 'He likes you, Cassie!'

'He's a charmer, is what he is.'

'Of course! Why not? His father owns half of your English West Country! You don't get more magical than that.' Isabella gave her a nudge and a wink.

'Well.' Cassie shook her head ruefully, still reeling from the impact of that smile. 'It's only one coffee, right? Where's the harm in that?'

CHAPTER FIVE

'What exactly are we supposed to be studying?'

Cassie tapped her spoon against her coffee cup, well aware she looked nervous. Richard leaned back in his chair.

'Life, Miss Bell. People. Culture.' He flung out an arm as if he was presenting her with the entire city. He probably could, she thought dryly.

'So it's not just a morning messing around or doing retail therapy?'

'Now, now. Sir Alric is big on self-motivation, initiative, that kind of guff. That's why I took you to the Pompidou Centre first, and the museum.' His face split in a grin. '*Now* we can mess around.'

'Oh. OK.'

The sun was warm on the back of her neck, and a light breeze played among the leaves of plane trees and the small zinc tables of the café. Traffic fumes mingled with strong scents of coffee and bread and someone's pungent French cigarette. Fidgeting, she picked up her cup, and put it down again. Empty.

'Let me get you another of those.' With what seemed barely more than a flicker of his eyelid and a twitch of one finger, Richard summoned a white-aproned waiter. 'Something to eat, Cassie?'

'Well, I—'

He didn't wait, but gave his order in clipped French, ending on a dazzling smile that even the surly waiter had to return. Replacing his customary scowl, the man turned and hurried away, as if embarrassed to have shown a spark of humanity.

'There's birds in that thar tree,' said Cassie, nodding at one of the plane trees in the square. 'Go on, charm them out of it, I dare you.'

Richard laughed in delight. 'I'd rather concentrate on charming you.'

Cassie searched his face for traces of mockery, but Richard met her stare full-on, smiling.

'Don't be so hung up on being a scholarship girl,' he said. 'You're much more interesting than all these spoilt heiresses and daughters of despots. Prettier too.'

'Oh, get a life.' Cassie felt herself flush scarlet. 'Or

did you mean I'm prettier than the despots?'

Richard hooted. 'I like you, Cassie Bell! You're a proper student, and you're funny too. Those other girls, they're comestibles.'

Cassie blinked. 'You lost me.'

'I could eat them in one bite.' He bared his white teeth.

'In your dreams, mate.'

Mind you, Cassie thought, he probably could take his pick of the girls at school. The combination of looks and charm was dizzying.

'Really, though, I'm serious. Those girls are gorgeous, sure, in a polished sort of way, but you're striking. Your eyes could pierce sheet metal, I swear to God. What do you call that colour? Green? They're so pale they're nearly yellow.'

Cassie fidgeted with her hair. 'I dunno. Ordinary?'

'Oh, anything but. And your bone structure is to die for.'

'Give over. I've got a pointy chin.'

'Just what I said. Amazing bone structure. You know who you look like? You're *really* like—'

'Like . . . ?'

But Richard had stopped himself in mid-flow, and was chewing the inside of his cheek.

'You're not *beautiful*,' he rushed on, giving the word a

deprecating emphasis. 'Not like the despotesses. You're more natural. Real. *Fresh*. Anyway,' he added conspiratorially, 'some of them don't even shave their armpits.'

The new coffees arrived at that moment, so Cassie had to put her hands over her mouth to stifle her explosion of laughter. The waiter gave her a filthy look.

'You are the limit,' she said when he'd gone. 'What's this?'

'*Pain au chocolat*. Go on, try it, it's heavenly.'

Doubtfully she bit into it. It was warm and flaky – like Richard, she thought with an inner grin – and entirely delicious. God, she hadn't realised how hungry she was. She didn't know if dunking it in her *café au lait* was the done thing, but what the hell: she dunked it anyway. As the melted chocolate hit her tongue she sighed blissfully.

Richard was watching her with amusement, and she remembered suddenly to be embarrassed. Honestly, she was eating like she hadn't seen food for a month. She made herself put the pastry down and take a swig of coffee.

'I like a girl with a healthy appetite,' he said archly.

Cassie threw her napkin at him. 'Aren't you hungry?'

'That's not really the sort of thing I like.' He ran a finger round the rim of his tiny cup of espresso. 'Although

Pain With Chocolate does sound very appealing.'

'That's not what it means,' Cassie told him. 'Even I know that. You are wicked.'

He raised a languid eyebrow. 'You have no idea.'

Cassie had to laugh again, shaking her head. What on earth was she doing here? she wondered again. Sitting in the Paris sunshine in a pavement café with a boy who was so far out of her league he might as well be in the next galaxy. 'Where are you from, then, devil boy?'

His grin flashed. 'Hades and Norfolk.' He took a sip of his thick black coffee.

'Oh? Isabella said something about the West Country.'

'Just because we own rather a lot of it doesn't mean we have to live there.'

The face of him. For the first time she felt a tingle of disapproval. She scowled. 'Is that how you got to join the Few?'

'Oh, Cassie, don't look at me like that, I beg you.' He made puppy eyes. 'I'm sorry if I offended you. I'm a rich spoilt brat and it sometimes shows. Of course, it's also a good qualification for joining the Few.'

'So that's why Isabella isn't one of you? I mean, she's rich and beautiful, but she's not a spoilt brat.'

'Cassie, your words cut me to the bone.' Dramatically, Richard clasped his hands over his heart. 'It's the truth that stings like a whiplash, I suppose.' He gave her another grin that melted her hostility. 'As for bella, bella Isabella, you never know. We're due to initiate another member this term, and the Few aren't all self-centred swines like me. She could be in with a chance. And if Isabella gets an invitation to the third floor, it won't be before time, in my humble opinion.'

'Has your opinion ever been humble?' Cassie still couldn't repress her smile, though her heartbeat had suddenly slipped up a gear. 'What's on the third floor?'

'Our common room. The Few's, I mean.'

'Really?' She took a casual sip of coffee. 'I bet that's something else. You couldn't let me see it, could you?'

'Tut tut!' Richard wagged a finger at her. 'Certainly not. What a temptress you are.' He smiled again. 'Not that special invitations haven't been known.'

'Go on. You've made me really curious.'

Cheekily, he tapped her nose with a forefinger. 'Invitations to the common room have to come from all the Few. Sorry, my dear, but it's a rule. I can't just take you up there.'

Cassie shrugged as if she couldn't care less. 'Law unto yourselves, you lot, aren't you? The Few. I mean, what kind of a name is that? What do you do, except skip classes? I mean, what are you *for*?' Her laughter came out a little strained.

Richard was watching her closely again, his smile a more thoughtful one.

'Coffee's cold.' He stood up, his zinc chair scraping on the flagstones, and glanced at the watch on his wrist. 'And study time's over. Heavens, Cassie, you're quite a distraction.' Carelessly he took her hand and drew her to her feet. 'Come along. Back to the Academy with you.'

CHAPTER SIX

'There you are, Cassie! How was the date? Come on, tell me all about it!'

Isabella was in the second-floor library, perched with Jake on a leather sofa the colour of polished conkers. Cassie wished she hadn't interrupted. Isabella had looked more animated than ever, touching Jake's arm, making him laugh, laughing back when he said something dark and droll. If she'd been in Isabella's position, Cassie would have resented anyone butting in, but the Argentinian clapped her hands and beckoned her over. Jake glanced her way too.

'Come *on*! What happened? Where did you go? What was Richard like?' Isabella patted the seat between her and Jake, but Cassie chose the arm instead. She didn't want to come between them and, anyway, she felt downright uncomfortable around Jake.

The way he looked at her was unnerving.

Did he know she'd trailed him the other night? Had he spotted her after all? She stared at the bookshelves that reached almost to the elaborate plasterwork of the ceiling. The only section of wall that wasn't covered in book spines was the massive gilt-framed mirror above the baroque fireplace. This room was as magnificent as the rest of the mansion, but who would ever find time to read all these books?

'Well, come on, give! Did Richard kiss you, Cassie?'

'Course he didn't kiss me!' Cassie shrugged, blushing. 'He was nice. Interesting. I like him.'

'M-hm.' Isabella dug her in the ribs. 'Where did you go?'

'Ow! First the Pompidou Centre. Then this gorgeous museum in the rue de Sévigné that used to be a private house. And finally his *perfect* little café,' she mimicked. 'On the rue de la Bastille.'

'Didn't they lock up aristocrats there?' muttered Jake. 'Best place for him. Watch that guy, Cassie.'

Cassie gave him a surprised look, but cheerfully Isabella leaned across and slapped his knee. 'Jake, don't be such a grouch. He took her to the musée Carnavalet! It's so romantic. So stunning.' She sighed. 'And so is Richard.'

'He's a stunning, romantic rat.' Jake obviously wasn't going to let it go.

'Hey, leave it out,' said Cassie lightly. 'You mean I can only attract rats?'

'Course not.' He grinned at her. 'But he's a charmer. Watch yourself, that's all.'

'He's a nice guy,' said Cassie, starting to feel a little cross. 'You can't judge him by his family. Or by what he's worth. I bet you wouldn't like that yourself.' Anyway, she thought, you're the one that needs watching.

Jake's face darkened. 'My family has nothing to do with this.'

'Well, maybe his hasn't either!'

'Jake, I know you don't like Richard, but there's no need,' put in Isabella soothingly. 'You mustn't have such a ship on your shoulder. You are just the same with Ranjit.'

Cassie had never actually seen someone's face freeze before. She'd thought it was just a figure of speech, but Jake's expression had gone rigid as stone. That look of hate didn't suit him. But that was what it was: hatred.

'Don't talk about him,' he hissed, then forced his features into something like a grin. 'And it's a *chip*, by the way.'

Isabella's startled breath had caught in her throat, but now she smiled with relief. 'Very well, I won't. Richard has nothing you haven't got. Nothing important.'

Her good humour seemed to have restored Jake's. 'Yeah, but I know how charming he can be. He tried it on with me once.'

Cassie did a double-take. 'He did?'

'Oh, sure. But he's not my type.'

Taken aback, she snapped, 'So that's why you don't like him?'

'Nah. I didn't mind him hitting on me, but he sure as hell minded me turning him down. He's had it in for me ever since.'

Isabella scowled at Jake. 'Now you're spoiling Cassie's date.'

'No, he isn't. That doesn't bother me.'

'Quite right. Richard Halton-Jones is a catch, Cassie!'

'Richard Halton-Jones is a love rat,' muttered Jake. 'And not just with girls.'

'You know what? I think you are very sweet to worry about Cassie. You don't *need* to, but it is very gallant of you.' Isabella leaned over again to kiss him on the cheek. Reddening, he gave her a sidelong, surprised grin.

'What a cosy little gathering,' said an icy voice.

Jake practically knocked Isabella off the sofa as he jumped up, his blush now almost thermonuclear. 'Katerina, I—'

The Swedish girl waved an elegant hand. 'No, Jake, I shan't interrupt. It's lovely that Isabella is getting some attention. Sometimes I think she lacks it.'

Yup: definitely more Snow Queen than Dancing Queen.

Katerina had chosen where to stand deliberately, Cassie decided, because she knew the light through the tall windows would flatter her pale skin. She'd picked the right backdrop, too: against the richly swagged dark-blue curtains she shone like a cold angel. Jake seemed bewitched. Isabella was thunderous.

'Katerina! Don't go,' pleaded Jake. 'We were just talking. Isabella was just being . . . enthusiastic.'

'Ah! Isabella is always enthusiastic. About *everything*! That's what I love about her! Dear Isabella, I think you understand life and love so much better than we do. Always such joy. Like a puppy!'

Katerina wore a delighted smile, but Cassie didn't miss the bite beneath her words. Isabella sucked in a breath, but even she had been silenced. Cassie looked expectantly at Jake, waiting for him to play the gallant again and leap to Isabella's defence. For a moment it seemed as if he might. Then he closed his mouth and gave Isabella a sheepish glance.

'Yeah, Isabella, I love how you enjoy life!' he said, too

brightly. He hovered for a moment, as if he might lean forward and kiss her back, but he was distracted by a discreet cough.

'Jake, be a darling.' Katerina turned to the floor-to-ceiling bookshelves and brushed her fingers across a set of leather spines. Jake shivered, as if it was his spine they'd stroked. 'I need the Voltaire, and the two volumes of Rousseau, but look at them, they are huge! I don't think I can manage on my own.'

'No problem, Katerina.' Reverently he drew the books out of the shelf and carried them after her. Cassie watched transfixed as they vanished into the corridor.

' "Ooh, can you carry my books, Jake?" Pah!' Isabella had got her voice back at last – a little late, thought Cassie ruefully. 'That boy will be horribly deformed by the time he leaves this school.'

'He will?' said Cassie.

'From being twisted round Katerina's little finger so often.' Isabella clenched her fists furiously. 'He is too stupid to know when he is being led by the nose. Like one of my father's bulls. Hah!'

'Don't worry. I don't think she really likes him. I mean, I think you're right, she's just stringing him along. She'll get fed up. He'll get over her.'

'Worry? Why would I worry? Why would I care

whether he gets over her, or throws himself into the Seine for love of her? I'm not interested in a boy whose brains are stuck in his—'

'Isabella!'

They laughed, and Isabella flung an arm round Cassie's shoulder. 'You're right, I know that. Poor Jake, he has been under her spell since he came to the Academy. Jake pines for Katerina, and Katerina pines for Ranjit Singh, so Jake won't ever have her. Serve him right.' She ended on rather a venomous note.

'Is that why Jake can't stand Ranjit? He looked practically homicidal when you mentioned him.'

'Oh. That.' Nervously Isabella chewed her knuckles, but after a moment she gathered her composure. 'Well. Love can do that to stupid boys. It's all hormones, of course. The relentless primitive drive of the sexual organs.'

'Cut it out!' giggled Cassie.

'That would be an extreme solution, but—'

Cassie gave a yelp of laughter. 'Stop it! So, seriously. Did Jake come on a scholarship too?'

'Yes. I think it saved him.' Isabella sighed, all softness and sympathy again. 'After his sister died, he went – what do you say? – off the rails? He went a bit crazy. A lot of trouble: fighting, gangs, drugs. Three high schools threw him out, but Sir Alric took an interest in his future, wanted to help him.'

Jake's sister died? So that was why he was so spiky. 'Nice of Sir Alric, but . . .' Cassie shrugged, then bit her lip. 'Why would he do that? I mean, Jake doesn't even seem that grateful.'

'Oh, but of course Sir Alric felt a responsibility! Jessica Johnson had a scholarship here before Jake did.'

'Oh, OK. So he kind of knew Jake through his sister?'

'He offered Jake a scholarship in his sister's memory. Sir Alric was right to do that, I think. It was a fine way to behave, whatever Jake says.' Isabella squeezed Cassie's arm, and lowered her voice. 'The school was where it happened.'

'Where what happened?' Cassie felt a chill in her spine.

'The accident. Jake's sister died at the Darke Academy.'

CHAPTER SEVEN

Cassie leaned on the ornate balustrade and stared down the west-wing staircase. This was where Ranjit had stood, watching her, three weeks ago. She tried to remember how afraid she'd been that night, but in daylight the staircase seemed only beautiful, not threatening. Below her, other students were hurrying down to the dining room, chattering and laughing easily. Out of the general chatter she heard Richard's abrupt, confident bark of laughter, and she smiled.

Still, she couldn't shake a niggling sense of wrongness.

As the noise and gossip faded, Cassie lingered, frowning. The balustrade was all black iron swirls, punctuated with gilt flourishes of feathers and suns. Glancing over her shoulder, she saw herself and the tall south-facing window reflected in an ornate gold mirror. You wouldn't think the place could seem so dark and sinister. Cassie shook her head.

She died at the Darke Academy. Jake's sister died . . .

At the Academy, in Cambodia. Isabella had been reluctant to explain, which was most unlike her. Cassie had had to badger her for days.

'I should not talk about it. Honestly, Cassie. A terrible thing. So very sad. Such a young death. And not the firs—'

Her roommate, uncharacteristically, had blushed and clamped her lips together, and no nagging from Cassie would persuade her to finish that sentence.

And not the first, either. Was that what she'd been about to say?

No. Could have been anything. Heck, Isabella could have been about to say, Not the first time somebody had an accident. Or, Not the first tragically young heart-attack victim.

But somehow Cassie didn't think it had been either of those.

'I don't know what happened.' Isabella had shrugged unhappily. 'We were never told details. It seemed . . . not right to ask, you know? There were rumours. There always are.'

Cassie had bitten her lip, hoping she didn't sound ghoulishly curious. 'What kind of rumours?'

'Oh, terrible things. People make things up, when there is no information. That is why I think we should have been told. Then gossip does not start.' Isabella had hesitated, picking at a fingernail. 'You look like her, by the way.'

'Like Jake's sister?' Cassie shivered. Resembling a dead girl was not an appealing thought.

'A little. Not exactly, of course, but her eyes were almost the colour of yours. Not so pale but still, that yellowish green. And a similar sort of face – how do you say, sharp? Intelligent. I think Jake got a fright when he first met you.'

She remembered. Spooky. 'So what were the rumours?'

'Oh, crazy things. That her body was . . . damaged.'

'*What?*' Cassie swallowed hard. 'Mutilated, you mean? Like she was killed deliberately?' Poor Jake.

'No, no. I don't know. Not mutilated. More . . . drained, dried-up. Maybe she cut herself, bled to death; that is what I think. By accident or not, who can tell? Something so simple and so tragic.'

'For God's sake. That wouldn't drain her whole body.'

Isabella shrugged. 'Maybe she lay in the sun too long. Before they found her, I mean. Horrible, but it was all exaggerated, I'm sure. Oh, the dreadful things people say. And that's why . . .'

'Why what? Come on Isabella, spill.'

Isabella sighed, raking her fingers through her hair. 'That's why Jake doesn't like Ranjit. Jess was Ranjit's girlfriend, you see. There were rumours at school that he was involved.'

Cassie went pale. 'But that's—'

'Crazy, of course! But it is hard for Jake to ignore the gossip. He cannot stop thinking that perhaps Ranjit . . . well, I don't even like to say it. It was a terrible accident, that is all, and Jake is grief-stricken. He cannot bear to blame it just on the school's bad luck.'

'Bad luck,' repeated Cassie, licking parched lips. *Dried-up* . . .

'Yes. Only bad luck. We are lucky Sir Alric has influential friends. Our parents, too. That is, I mean . . .' Biting her lip, she blushed furiously and rushed on. 'Such incidents can destroy a school, yes?'

'Such incidents.' At some point, thought Cassie, she would think of something original to say, instead of echoing Isabella like a dazed parrot.

'Accidents, I should say. Another one a few years ago. Before that . . . well. Let's not talk about it, Cassie. Let's talk about Richard!'

Which, by that point in the conversation, Cassie had been more than happy to do.

83

Still, it wasn't like Isabella to clam up. Hah! Great Understatements of Our Time, thought Cassie fondly. Oh, she was probably imagining things. Being paranoid. She wasn't having any miraculous revelations just by standing on the stairs, anyway. Plus, she was hungry. Isabella would be in the dining room, and Richard too. She was supposed to be meeting him later, but it would be nice to bump into him now.

She was halfway down the flight of stairs to the third floor when she heard the voices. They weren't muted. They rang out clear and confident, and she recognised them straight away.

Especially Richard's.

'Oh, come along, Katerina. It's not like you to be insecure.'

'Insecure?' The voice froze Cassie where she stood, there was such malevolence in it. 'I can't think what you mean, Richard.'

A hidden door closed sharply, and Cassie jumped. The pair were in that long corridor with the rows of classical busts, the one where she'd tracked down Jake. The one that led to the Few's common room, she realised with a jolt.

Giving its archway an anxious glance, Cassie ran down the stairs to the landing and ducked behind a marble-topped cabinet. An enormous gilded clock and two candelabra obscured her view, but she could peer past, just.

Mad, thought Cassie, almost laughing. Why was she hiding? It was only Richard. And Katerina, of course, but it wasn't as if she was scared of the Polar Rottweiler. Still, when they appeared at the end of the corridor, she didn't saunter out to say hello. Not yet. Those instincts kicking in again . . .

'Darling, she's a chav from the sticks.' Folding his arms, Richard raised an ironic eyebrow at Katerina. 'You don't actually feel threatened, do you?'

Cassie's whole body went rigid. For a moment she couldn't breathe.

' "A *chav* from the *sticks*." What a quaint turn of phrase you have, Richard.' Katerina sounded immensely bored. 'That poor-little-scholarship-girl thing. How it vexes me. Such a mooning little kitten. Yet you seem to have a soft spot for her.'

'Don't be silly, Katerina darling. She's pleasant company and I find her amusing. So do you, if you're honest.'

'Oh, hilarious.' Katerina sniffed.

'I'm not the only one with a *soft spot*, either,' murmured Richard. 'Jake can barely let her out of his sight, if you see what I'm getting at.'

'Oh, yes. His protective instincts,' said Katerina contemptuously. 'She's very like poor little Jessica, it's true.'

'Doesn't that worry you?' There was mischief in his tone. 'Jessica was good-looking too.'

'Why would it worry me?' she snapped. 'Ranjit had a silly crush on a girl who was beneath him. And that ended in tears, didn't it?' Her lips twitched as she checked herself in the nearest mirror. 'He's hardly likely to make the same mistake again.'

'That's what I love about you.' Richard winked. 'Such perennial optimism.'

Katerina shot him a baleful glare. 'And that creature from the cattle farms encourages her to think above herself. Good God, darling, you'd think Isabella could at least encourage her to get a hairstyle and some decent clothes. Your "chav" can't even *pronounce* Versace. She wouldn't know Prada from Primark.'

'Perhaps bella Isabella could give her some hand-me-downs.' Richard chuckled. 'No wonder Sir Alric hides in his office. I mean, one fairly dreads to think what the likes of Cassie Bell or Jake Johnson will wear to the Christmas Ball. The poorhouse rejects do nothing for the aesthetics of the place, do they?'

They were obviously planning to linger and bitch

before heading downstairs, and Cassie could hear every word. She wished she couldn't. Her cheeks burned with shame and fury, and she ached to leap out, grab a throat in each fist and tell these tossers what she thought of them. But something held her back.

Idly, Katerina twisted a lock of pale satiny hair. 'I can't think why Sir Alric encourages this scholarship nonsense.'

'Now, now, darling,' said Richard darkly. 'You know very well why. Besides, it's excellent public relations. A fine pickle we'd be in if Sir Alric wasn't so skilled in that department.'

Even mired in miserable rage and embarrassment – *how could I have been so stupid!* – Cassie found herself intrigued. There was something wrong here. It wasn't her imagination. The picture-perfect world of the Academy hid something very ugly: she was sure of it.

The same could be said for the beautiful faces of Richard and Katerina.

Something hot stung her eyes, and she gritted her teeth. To hell with that. He wasn't going to make her cry. He was a male Katerina: stringing her along the way Katerina dangled Jake. She was humiliated, that was all.

Richard had turned at the top of the stairs, grinning back at Katerina. 'Aren't you hungry?'

'Starving, darling. But I think I shall miss lunch. What about you?'

Richard gave that sudden bark of laughter again. 'You know, I rather fancy a Danish.'

'Do stay away from Ingrid.' Katerina's look was sharkish, if amused. 'She's my roommate. If Sir Alric could hear you . . .'

'No sense of humour, that's his trouble.' With a giggle of delight, Richard jogged down the stairs.

Katerina stayed put for a long moment, unmoving, her eyes flickering to the mirror. Cassie stood very still.

Katerina gave herself one last reflected smile, turned, and disappeared back down the bust-lined corridor. Cassie didn't dare move until she heard the door open and close softly once more. Then she bolted.

She couldn't face the dining room: the red silk walls, the linen and crystal, the hubbub of gossip. She couldn't face the sly sidelong looks of the other students. Sickeningly, she realised she needn't have bothered struggling to learn which bloody fork to use: they'd always despise her, always. God, did every one of them know what a fool she'd made of herself? *Fool, Cassie!* Being dazzled by white teeth, warm eyes and a slick line in patter. She couldn't even face Isabella or Jake.

Recoiling, she sidled down the passageway and slunk

out of the French windows. Her eyes stinging again as she ran between two great stone urns, she took a flight of curved steps two at a time and stumbled across the expanse of lawn to the shadow of mature chestnut trees. Already tinged with autumn, the trees were beautiful. Growling, she punched one of them, hard. Then she hit it again. And again.

That felt better. Not much, but at least her sore knuckles took her mind off her bruised pride. That was what it was, she thought. Not a broken heart. Just her stupid, cracked pride. Who did she think she was, trying to impress an upper-class jerk like Richard Halton-Jones? Miserably she clasped her grazed fist, then lifted it to rub away a stray tear. The gold-and-bronze trees were splashed with sunlight, animated like an Impressionist painting. Staring at them, she wished more than anything she was back with the weed-choked yard, the rusty wire and the pitted brown grass of Cranlake Crescent. Just thinking about it made her vision blur.

A different shape came into her distorted view, moving purposefully across the lawn. Tall and humanoid. Oh, hell. As it came under the shade of the equally blurred tree-shapes, the figure stopped dead. Aghast, Cassie rubbed her eyes clear and blinked.

Not just hell, double-hell.

Ranjit.

For a moment he stood nonplussed, staring at her. Furious at herself, she blinked again. The gorgeous Ranjit. Oh, God, how typical: this was the first time in weeks he'd seen far enough past his princely nose to notice her, and here she was with red eyes, a blocked nose and a scowl like a moody harpy.

He looked her up and down. 'What's wrong?'

'Nothing,' she snapped. 'I'm fine.' *Why are you biting his head off, Cassie?*

'You don't look it. What's the problem?'

'There's no problem.' She clenched her fists. 'Or nothing I can't handle. I don't need your help.'

His stare was unswerving. It made her shiver.

'Don't be too sure of that.'

Not knowing what to say, she could only glare back at him, breathing hard. You can take the girl out of Cranlake Crescent, she thought bitterly, but you can't take Cranlake Crescent out of the girl. His sheer beauty didn't make him worth trusting: look at Richard. She had to keep her guard up. The last half-hour's humiliation stung *so much*.

'I'm going to give you a piece of advice,' he said.

'Whether I want it or not?'

'Yes.' Ranjit's eyes were cold. 'Stay away from Richard Halton-Jones.'

'I've worked that out for myself, thanks,' she spat.

'Oh. I see.' He grimaced. 'I'm sorry.'

'Please don't be. Just sod off.' Cassie bit hard on her lip, desperate not to burst into tears in front of him.

'Fine, if you do me a favour too. In fact, do yourself a favour. Stay away from all of us.'

'I'm not good enough for the precious Few, is that it?'

'Oh, get down from your high horse before you fall off. Listen, if you get involved with the Few, you'll regret it.'

Cassie felt blood creep hotly up her neck and throat. 'Are you threatening me?'

'No. I'm warning you.'

'And how the hell is it your business to warn me?'

'I've made it my business, Cassandra.'

The way he spoke her name he almost sounded concerned, but when she looked up to his face it was a study in inscrutability. Jerk.

'Well, you can just unmake it, then. I don't need your advice, or your warnings. And I *really* don't need you stalking me around the corridors at night.'

Ranjit's eyes widened, and Cassie gave an inward smirk. He hadn't been expecting that.

'I wasn't—' He shrugged and smiled a strange, bitter smile. 'Well, if you're so perfectly self-sufficient, I won't waste my time worrying about you.'

In disbelief, Cassie watched him stride off across the lawn. He didn't so much as glance back, the stuck-up tosser. He could go screw himself. 'Cos obviously no one else would ever be good enough.

Cassie slumped down against the trunk of the tree, still staring after him.

She'd never met such a horse's arse in her life.

And she fancied him like crazy.

CHAPTER EIGHT

Cassie's eyes snapped open. Must have been a nightmare. Rubbing her arms, she stared at the stirring curtains and listened to the moonlit silence. She had lain awake until well past midnight, cringing inwardly about Richard. So the hard and streetwise Cassie Bell had fallen for a bit of chinless charm? Pathetic.

Not that he was actually chinless. Hell of a handsome, really. But all of it skin-deep. And there was a good chance that the rest of these rich bráts were the same. So she should stop letting Ranjit creep into her brain the way he did.

She was sure he had been part of the nightmare that had just woken her, though she couldn't remember the details. It had dissolved as she woke, but she could still sense a pair of night-eyes branded on the inside of her eyelids. And silence was always so ominous coming out of a nightmare, though she could hear the echo of an imagined whisper.

No. That wasn't an echo, and she hadn't imagined it. That really was a whisper. Cassie swung her legs off the bed and held herself still.

Soft footfalls. Even softer voices.

As usual, Isabella was sleeping like a sedated baby. Cassie almost wanted to shake her awake, but she resisted the temptation. She could stay in bed herself. She *should* stay in bed. What she ought to do now was pull the soft bedclothes over her head, blot out those whispering voices and go back to sleep. What she really, really ought to do was mind her own business . . .

Uh-huh.

Isabella's long cashmere cardigan was slung over a chair. Dragging it round her shoulders, Cassie pulled open the door. It was still October, and though it wasn't cold she shivered as she stepped cautiously into the corridor. Jake again? This time she'd confront him. This time she'd find out what he was up to.

It wasn't Jake.

Cassie pressed herself against the wall. Two girls were walking silently towards the west wing, and she'd know one of those silhouettes anywhere: small and perfectly formed, with a black razored haircut. Keiko.

The girl with her was a little taller, and fair-haired. It took Cassie a moment to recognise her, since her hair was usually bound up in a chic knot: Alice, Keiko's roommate. As the light from a wall sconce fell on the pair, Cassie saw that Keiko's fingers were locked round Alice's wrist. She wasn't dragging Alice, exactly, but Alice didn't seem too thrilled to be going along with her.

Cassie frowned.

'Keiko.' Alice's whisper drifted back through the silent corridor. 'I don't like this.' She jerked Keiko to a halt.

Keiko turned to face her roommate, watching her silently for a moment. Cassie shrank further into the wall.

'I told you before,' murmured Keiko silkily. 'It's a request from the Few. You can't say no. Come on, Alice. What could possibly happen?'

'I don't know. I don't— What happened last time? I mean, I don't remember.'

Keiko tightened her fingers on Alice's wrist and tugged her on. 'That's because you had too much to drink. Believe me, you had a great time.'

'I did?'

'Of course. Do come on, it's a privilege. Late-night drinks in the Few's common room? There are girls in this school who'd kill for the chance you're getting.'

'Yeah? So why me?'

'You're lucky to have me as a roommate, that's all.' Keiko gave her a smile that Cassie didn't like one bit, even at a distance. But Alice seemed reassured.

'Well, don't let me drink too much this time, all right?'

'OK, I'll try not to, either.' Keiko's tone became more insistent. 'What do you remember, anyway? From last time.'

'Just being there. Lots of talking. Having a drink. Not much after that.' Alice shrugged and almost giggled. 'I didn't realise I'd drunk so much.'

'I'll look after you.' Squeezing her arm, Keiko smiled. 'Don't worry about that.'

Letting her roommate go, Keiko turned to carry on as if she didn't care whether Alice came with her or not. Alice hesitated only for a moment, then scuttled after her.

Following them, Cassie stayed well back. There was no way she wanted Keiko to spot her, and she knew where they were going. Keiko padded purposefully to the west-wing staircase, then led Alice up to the third floor and into the corridor where the blank-eyed busts stood guard like watchful ghosts.

Cassie edged towards the archway, risking a glance round the corner. At the end of the corridor, the shadows deepened, but a line of greenish light showed at the bottom of the door. Keiko didn't knock. She turned the handle and drew Alice after her into the common room.

Cassie exhaled with relief. What now? She couldn't just stand there till they came back out. On the other hand, if she crept back to bed she wouldn't sleep anyway. This was her only chance to investigate, and she was damned if she was passing it up. *Go on, Cassie*. Clenching her fists, she made herself put one foot in front of the other. And again. *Come on*. She could hear the muted clink of crystal now, and soft murmuring voices. It hardly sounded like a wild midnight party, but the door was thick, the sounds muffled. She had to get closer.

A flash at the corner of her eye almost made her cry out. In the darkness of those deeper recesses by the door, something had moved.

Cassie froze. As her eyes adjusted, she could make it out. A figure, a human figure.

Jake Johnson. Of course.

The light had glanced off his watch and, as she made herself creep towards him, she saw his fingers clasped over his wrist to hide it. He'd realised.

Raising her eyes, she met his. He was expressionless, but the tiny jerk of his head was clear enough. *Bugger off and go back to bed . . .*

Then something distracted him, and he retreated into the alcove.

Footsteps. She heard them too. And there was no way out of here.

The footfalls were on the landing now. She couldn't slip out of the corridor without being seen. She could run to Jake, slip in and hide with him. But then Cassie thought about his eerily purposeful nocturnal prowling. Did she want to be with him in the silent dark, afraid of discovery, completely at his mercy?

No, she decided. Digging her fingernails into the palms of her hands, taking a deep scared breath, Cassie spun on her heel.

At the entrance to the corridor, a man came to an abrupt halt. She'd only ever seen his portrait – and that didn't do him justice, she decided. His steel-grey eyes were fixed on her, the only light in a face of stone. He couldn't really have been seven feet tall, but that was the impression he gave. Hairs prickled on her neck as if responding to an electric field of power.

Sir Alric Darke smiled. 'Cassie Bell.'

She smiled back, the brightest and dumbest smile she could manage. 'That's right. Hi.' She flapped the fingers of one hand in a feeble greeting.

'You seem to be lost, and it's very late. May I help you?'

Nerve-janglingly aware of Jake behind her, Cassie stepped closer to Sir Alric. His eyes flickered past her.

She stepped in front of him, determined to keep his attention. 'Could you, please? No sense of direction, me.'

He gave a gentle laugh. 'It's rather a big place, isn't it? I'll find someone to escort you back. I'm Alric Darke, by the way.'

'I know. Yes. I mean,' Cassie cleared her throat, keeping her smile in place, 'I've seen your picture.'

His hand clasped her elbow and he guided her to the door of the common room. He seemed kind, but there was that force field around him, of command and potential threat. As they passed the hidden Jake, Cassie kept her gaze fixed on the door, scared of giving him away.

Sir Alric swung open the door, and drew Cassie into the room.

The light was muted, but the common room seemed as elegant as the rest of the Academy. She had an impression of dark-red leather armchairs, baroque lamps, elaborate panelling and paintings rich with colour. She glimpsed people she knew, too: Katerina, Keiko, a Russian sixth former from her fencing class. Richard seemed surprised to see her. There were others, too, from the beautiful Few, but no Ranjit.

And there was Alice on an upright gilded chair, a silver cup in her hands, rigid and stupefied.

'Keiko.' Sir Alric's voice was calm, but icy with menace.

The Japanese girl swung round, face paler than usual.

'What is Alice doing here?'

'She . . . that is, I—'

'Roommates', he hissed, 'should be respected.'

'I was only—'

'And I should be informed of all late-night meetings. Should I not?'

Meekly she said, 'Of course, Sir Alric. I'm sorry.'

Much as Cassie disliked Keiko, Sir Alric seemed to be overreacting big time to a midnight feast. His fingers on her arm were like steel.

'Katerina.' He spoke silkily. 'Clear up in here. When I return in ten minutes, I want everyone gone. You, at least, should know better. Keiko: come with us, please. Cassie is lost. You will show her the way back.'

Keiko stood up from her place beside Alice, giving Cassie a glance of the utmost loathing which melted into a sweet smile for Sir Alric. 'Of course.'

Cassie expected Sir Alric to leave her to Keiko's tender mercies, but he followed them out, stopping to close the door. Cassie snatched a glance into Jake's alcove. It was empty. He'd obviously made good his escape while they'd been inside the common room.

'Cassie, please wait for us at the end of the corridor. Keiko, you can stay here for a moment.'

With one vicious glance at Cassie, Keiko hung back. Embarrassed, and even a little sorry for her, Cassie walked away.

Maybe Sir Alric didn't realise how good her hearing was, honed sharp from spying on Jilly Beaton. Cassie was sure he didn't mean her to overhear the bollocking he was giving Keiko, ten metres away. His voice was soft, but homicidal.

'*Sharing is forbidden!*'

'*I know, Sir Alric, but—*'

'*Consider this your last warning, Keiko. There are good reasons you are assigned a roommate. Understand?*'

'*Yes, Sir Alric. I understand.*'

Without another word he turned on his heel and strode to Cassie's side, Keiko trailing sulkily behind him.

'I'm sorry I haven't made a point of meeting you before now, Cassie.' Sir Alric's voice was no longer ferocious and chilly: it was lovely, she thought. Resonant like music. 'I find myself constantly tied up in administrative matters.'

'Oh yeah, don't worry. You're a big improvement on Jilly Beaton.' She blushed. 'In Cranlake Crescent, I mean. Where I was before.'

Behind them, Keiko was silent, though Cassie could feel her contempt oozing over her like tar.

'Of course,' said Sir Alric after a heavy pause. 'This

must be quite a culture shock for you, but I believe you are fitting in very well. I hear good things from your teachers, and from the Few. We are delighted to have you here at the Darke Academy, Cassie, delighted.'

'Um,' she muttered awkwardly, 'great. Thanks.'

'And are you happy here?'

He had turned his head, and she felt obliged to look up at him. He really was an amazing man. Must be knocking sixty, but still good-looking, and his charisma could blast you into the middle of next week.

She smiled. 'Yes. Oh, it's . . . amazing. Yes, of course I love it.' Funnily enough, she realised, that was absolutely true.

'Good. That's good.' He nodded. 'Is there anything that concerns you? Any . . . worries?'

Cassie shrugged, averting her eyes. 'Um. No. Should there be?' Stupid remark, she thought, giving herself a mental kick.

But Sir Alric either didn't hear it, or pretended that he hadn't. 'I'm glad. I do encourage students to come to me with any problems, no matter how trivial. You will remember that, Cassie, won't you?' He gave her another smile, so radiant and infectious she could only return it. 'Some students find me a little . . . unapproachable. Somewhat remote. That's my fault, of course, but I don't want you to feel that way. Feel free to come to my office at any time, Cassie – if you have questions, if you need to ask for help or advice. That's why I'm here.'

They'd come to the bottom of the west-wing staircase now, and he steered her along the corridor. Keiko still hadn't spoken, but her silence was a furious one. She was simmering, but it was impossible to tell if Sir Alric had noticed. Cassie was glad he was between them. She felt safer with him there, so her heart plummeted when they emerged into the grand entrance hall and Sir Alric halted.

'Keiko will show you back to your room.'

'Oh, I don't need . . . I'm fine now, I can manage on my own.'

He tutted and laughed. 'I'd worry. That sense of direction of yours! Please, Cassie, let Keiko take you back.'

'But . . . OK.' Cassie glanced at Keiko, but the girl was glaring into space.

'I'm glad to have met you at last. You're going to be an asset to the Academy, I know that. You fit in here as if you were born to it.' He took her hand. 'Take care, Cassie.' His voice chilled. 'Keiko. My office. First thing tomorrow.'

Keiko was silent till his footsteps had faded. Then Cassie heard her murmur, so soft she wasn't even sure if Keiko was talking to her, 'Do you know who all the statues are?'

Was she actually trying to be chatty? Taken aback, Cassie shook her head. 'Achilles?' she said doubtfully. 'And I recognised Leda and the Swan in the courtyard.'

Keiko made a contemptuous face. 'The Swan is Zeus in disguise, doing as he likes with a mere mortal.'

'I know that,' said Cassie, irritated at the patronising tone. 'And that one's Hermes, right?'

'Yes.' Keiko, uninterested in Hermes, turned to a stag that was rearing in motionless terror, marble hounds tearing at its haunches. A beautifully sculpted woman looked on, disdainful.

There was a chill in the air, thought Cassie. 'So who's that?'

'Artemis. The hunting goddess,' said Keiko, sounding amused. 'The stag is Actaeon, a hunter who dared to spy on her as she bathed. Artemis turned him into a stag as a punishment. And then his own hounds tore him to pieces.'

The silence was thick with menace. No, Keiko definitely wasn't trying to be friendly.

The girl gave an unnerving chuckle. 'Oh, it's only a *myth*. A warning from the ancients. Gods should not be treated lightly, you see? Gods should not be mocked. I mean, take this little tragedy . . .'

Almost against her will, Cassie found herself following

Keiko across the hall, to where one marble woman cowered at the feet of another. The supplicant had lifted one pathetic hand, to shield herself or to plead for mercy. The woman above her, axe poised to strike, didn't look like she knew the meaning of the word.

'This is your namesake, did you know?' Keiko touched the pleading marble hand. 'Cassandra. Do you know about Cassandra's curse?'

Cassie shook her head, not trusting herself to speak.

'She was a prophetess. Ever so fine and clever, because her prophecies always came true.' Keiko sniffed. 'Cassandra was never wrong. Oh, yes, she always knew when something terrible was going to happen. But no one would ever believe her.' Her smile was very unpleasant. 'No one.'

Cassie cleared her throat. 'That's a bummer.'

'Isn't it just? This is Clytaemnestra, who murdered her when Agamemnon brought her back from Troy. Cassandra knew that would happen, too. She refused to enter the palace, screaming that she smelled blood.'

'I see.' Cassie's heart beat furiously. 'And nobody believed that either?'

'Nobody believed that either.' Keiko shook her head with mock sadness. 'And so she entered the palace.' She nodded at Clytaemnestra's axe. 'And got what was coming to her.'

'Poor old Cassandra,' said Cassie, keeping her voice level.

'Indeed.' Keiko sighed, but then something seemed to snap inside her. 'Well, let's not waste any more time.'

'I don't need your help,' said Cassie stiffly. 'Don't bother coming with me. I won't tell Sir Alric.'

'You are *too* kind. As is he,' hissed Keiko.

'Oh, yeah?'

'Yeah. You don't fit in, *Cassandra*. You think you're so clever, don't you?' All her mock courtesy had dissolved, and she snorted with contempt. 'You're an exercise in public relations, and don't you ever forget it. You're here for our benefit, not the other way round.'

Cassie clenched her fists to stop herself slapping Keiko. *Don't lose it, Cassie. That's what she wants.* 'What's his problem, anyway? Why's Alice not allowed in the common room?' Sarcastically she added, '*Few business*, is it?'

Keiko didn't answer. Backing off a step, then two, she reached out a hand to stroke the flank of the terrified stag. Her fingers trailed across the cold marble to caress the snarling muzzle of one of the hunting dogs. Cassie shuddered. It was some carving. The fangs looked as if they were sunk in real flesh.

'Keep out of it, Cassie Bell, if you know what's good for

you.' Keiko turned on her heel, then tucked her glossy hair behind her ear and smiled back at Cassie.

'And sleep well.'

CHAPTER NINE

'Never mind statues.' Isabella stood with her arms folded and an expression of thrilled determination on her face. 'That's what I call a *proper* Hermès.'

'You do my head in.' Cassie raised her eyebrows. 'You could buy a small country for that price.'

Isabella stroked the soft, buttery leather of the bag. 'And what would I want with a small country? Let me buy you one too, Cassie! It will never let you down. It is not an indulgence, it is an investment!'

'A small country?'

Isabella dug her in the ribs, so hard that Cassie's giggle came out in a gasp. 'A Hermès bag, you *philistine*.'

'Uh-uh. No way.' Rubbing her side, Cassie shook her head firmly. 'I'm happy with the one I've got.'

Not strictly true – six months on she still felt guilty about shoplifting it – but she liked her chainstore bag all the same. Anyway, she wasn't going to start letting Isabella buy her stuff. She'd have a string of polo ponies before she knew it, and where would she put them? She grinned.

'What's so funny? *Oui*,' Isabella told the assistant imperiously. 'I'll take it, please. *Vous* accept this card, yes? *Merci* so very *beaucoup*.'

'Your French is diabolical,' Cassie told her as Isabella flipped her credit card on to the desk. 'Better than mine, though.'

'Not true. And mine serves my purposes anyway! Come along, shopping makes me terribly hungry. I'm buying lunch and don't you *dare* argue. What was it you wanted to ask me?'

Reluctant to talk in front of the haughty high-priestesses of the boutique, Cassie waited till they were out of the door, and inside a restaurant on the avenue Montaigne. She slunk into the seat she was shown, awkward again. This place was even posher than the Academy's dining room. Trendier, too.

'Let's have the *poule au pot*. It's wonderful.' Isabella gave the waiter a dazzling smile and returned the massive menu so enthusiastically it flew like a frisbee. 'Come along, Cassie. Out with it. You have been a cat in a hot tin bath all morning.'

'*On* a hot tin *roof*,' said Cassie. 'You nearly decapitated a waiter.'

'Do not change the subject.' Isabella wagged a finger.

'Isabella.' She hesitated. 'Why would anyone go to the Few's common room in the middle of the night?'

Opening her elegant shopping bag, Isabella peered into it with a smile of satisfaction. 'I don't know. Forgot their books? Meeting a boyfriend?'

'No.' Cassie tapped her fingernails on the table. 'It was some sort of gathering. At two o'clock in the morning.'

'Really?' Isabella fiddled with her new purchases, distracted. 'They have Congresses at strange times sometimes. Don't worry.'

'It can't have been a Congress. Sir Alric didn't know about it. He turned up and he was furious. Oh, and anyway, Alice was there?'

Isabella was suddenly all ears. '*Alice?*'

'You know, Keiko's—'

'Yes, yes, of course. But *Alice?*' Isabella sounded sulky. 'Why her?'

'Just what I'd like to know.'

'It's obvious, isn't it? They want to enrol her. Make her a member,' said Isabella in a voice tinged with bitterness. 'Oh yes, Alice will suit the vacancy very nicely.'

Cassie stopped drumming and clasped her fingers

110

together. 'I don't think so. They weren't interviewing her for the Few. I'd take a bet on it.'

'It is all the same to me, you know. I am not concerned. There is no need to try to make me feel better.'

'No. No, I swear I'm not. I'm just sure that wasn't why she was there. It was the way they—'

'Sh!' Straightening in her chair, Isabella patted her hand urgently. 'Stop. Don't say any more.'

Following the none-too-subtle jerk of Isabella's head, Cassie found herself pinned by an icy blue gaze.

Three tables away sat Katerina Svensson and three older girls, sixth formers. Katerina didn't smile, and neither did Cassie.

'Did it just get colder in here?' She nudged Isabella and giggled, but the laughter died on her lips as the restaurant door opened again. 'Oh, *hell*. It's *him*. No! Isabella, don't look!'

Too late. Isabella's whole face brightened as she waved. 'Jake. Hey, Jake!'

'Can you act a bit cooler yourself?' muttered Cassie. 'Hard to get, that kind of thing?'

'But I'm not,' Isabella said mischievously. 'Not where he is concerned. Hey, *Jake*!'

But Jake Johnson, thought Cassie, had no chance of getting to their table. Poor Isabella. Katerina had turned, laying a delicate hand on Jake's arm as he passed, smiling up beguilingly.

'Jake, *darling*.'

Cassie could read Katerina's lips, though she couldn't hear her over the lunchtime murmur of voices. The Swedish girl cast a sly sneer at Isabella as Jake came to a besotted halt. Leaning down, he kissed her proffered cheek and said something. Katerina laughed and clasped his fingers, and Cassie waited with a sinking heart for Jake to sit down and wrap an arm round her.

He didn't. Cassie frowned, surprised. Smiling, Jake straightened, and released the Swedish girl's hand. Katerina's smirk evaporated as Jake turned away, towards Cassie and Isabella. Cassie had to put her hand over her mouth to hide her grin of delight. That expression on Katerina's face? She wanted to cast it in marble for posterity, and stick it on a bust in the entrance hall.

'Hi, Isabella. Hi, Cassie.' Jake yanked out a chair and sat down. 'Isabella, you haven't been shopping *again*? Did Daddy mortgage the ranch?'

Isabella punched his arm. 'You wound me, Jake. Always, you wound me.'

'Speaking as the Kettle, Miss Pot, I find that remark pretty ironic. Whatcha bought?'

Cheeks pink with pleasure, Isabella lifted her bag and

opened it for his inspection. As he examined the contents, Cassie looked to the side again.

'Does your back hurt?' she said dryly. ''Cos it's full of daggers.'

'Huh?' Jake turned, but Katerina had swiftly averted her venomous stare. He scratched his neck, blushing. 'Oh. Katerina. She's OK.' His hawkish features melted into a helpless smile. 'Well. Incredible, actually.'

'Incredible,' muttered Cassie. 'You got that right. I wonder where her pal Keiko is.'

'In detention,' said Jake, winking at Cassie with wicked satisfaction. 'She was called to Sir Alric's office this morning. Got an absolute rocket, apparently.'

'Really?' said Cassie, feigning surprise. So Sir Alric hadn't quite finished with the wretched girl last night? She couldn't help grinning, though. 'Poor Keiko.'

'Oh dear. Sir Alric does get annoyed sometimes, even with the Few.' Isabella managed to sound concerned. 'And is Katerina upset that you are sitting with us?'

'Nah. Why would she be upset? I just wanted to talk to you . . . guys.'

Cassie heard the slight hesitation, and realised Jake was entirely focused on her. She gave him a frown. Not only did the boy have a sinister sleepwalking habit, he had about as much tact as Katerina. Deliberately she smiled at

Isabella, not Jake. 'Yeah? What about?'

'Actually, Cassie, I wondered if I could have a . . . word?'

Cassie wondered if her foot would reach far enough to give him a good hard kick. 'With us? Course you can. What do you want?'

'Well, I . . .' He fidgeted, half-turning towards Isabella.

Cassie saw the flush creep up Isabella's throat and darken her face. Abruptly, the Argentinian stood up, her linen napkin crushed in her fist. 'I'm sorry. I am being obtuse. Of course, it is something private.' She bent down to kiss Cassie's cheeks and snatched up her shopping bags. 'You know, I am not so hungry. I'll see you back at school, Cassie.' Managing one over-bright smile, she turned and walked out of the restaurant.

Cassie couldn't miss Katerina's satisfied smirk.

'That was really rude,' she hissed, standing up sharply. 'I'm going with her. You've got anything to ask me, you can ask in front of my friend.'

His fingers gripped her wrist. 'Cassie, please. *Please.*'

'Get stuffed.'

'I'm sorry, OK?' His voice was a desperate whisper. 'Listen, I'll make it up to her. I swear I'll apologise. *Please* stay, Cassie. This is important. Really important.'

She scowled at him. 'You'll make it up to her?'

'Yeah. Um, yeah, I promise.'

Cassie gave him a hard smile. 'Flowers.'

'What?' He blinked.

'Flowers. That's the only way to apologise to a girl. Don't you know anything?'

'Flowers?'

Bitchy inspiration struck. He really ought to pay for this. 'Make it an orchid. A *good* orchid.'

'OK, OK, I promise. Now will you listen to me?'

'Five minutes,' she snapped. 'And let go of me.'

He released her wrist, as if shocked he was still holding it. 'What were you up to last night, Cassie?'

She hesitated, surprised by his directness, then sat back down. 'Isn't that kind of a personal question?'

'Come on, please. Don't play games. This is serious.'

'Yeah? How serious?'

Picking up a fork, he turned it over and over in his fingers. 'Cassie, what were you doing on the third floor last night?'

'Sleepwalking. I guess it's a common habit, right?'

There was an awkward pause.

'Look, I . . .' He took a breath. 'I'm only—'

'Yeah? You're only what? What's *your* game, Jake?' She couldn't suppress a furious sneer. 'Are you that desperate to follow the Snow Queen around?'

115

He dropped the fork back on to the linen tablecloth. 'Cassie, I know it looks weird, but I swear I'm not doing anything wrong. Please, will you just tell me why you were there?'

'Not till you do, sunshine.'

'All right.' He ran his hands across his scalp. 'Will you just tell me this? I know Darke tore a strip off Keiko, but what did he say to you?'

'Not much.' She shrugged, scanning the room for a distraction. Where the hell was that waiter?

Jake wasn't letting it go. 'Did he— Was he threatening?'

'Of course not. Don't be ridiculous.'

'What about Ranjit?'

'*What?* What about him?'

'Did *he* threaten you? In the common room, I mean. Did he say anything?'

Cassie hesitated. *But he wasn't there, Jake . . .*

Thoughtfully she bit her lip. There was no reason to lie to Jake. But there was no reason to trust him, either. 'No,' she said at last. 'Ranjit didn't threaten me either. Why would he?'

Jake didn't answer. He seemed troubled.

'I need to go now. I hope you're fond of chicken, 'cos you've got two mains to get through.' She stood up. 'And pay for.'

He looked as if he might grab her wrist again, but managed to restrain himself. 'Cassie, will you please be careful? *Really* careful?'

'You certainly are a patronising git, aren't you?'

'Maybe.' Jake grinned, just. 'But I'm serious.'

'So am I. Don't you dare hurt my friend's feelings again.'

'Round here?' He gave her a thin-lipped smile. 'I'm not the one who does the hurting.'

Cassie turned on her heel, throwing Katerina a last ferocious glower. She could feel the girl's loathing, and Jake's stare, so she walked out very carefully. Now would be the worst time in the world to trip over her own feet.

Parisian elegance, she told herself grimly. And pride. *I'm a student at the Academy, dammit!*

She wasn't going to let them forget it.

CHAPTER TEN

Cassie focused intently on the art master. The class had left the Orangerie and its treasures, and now they sat blinking in the sunlight as Signor Poldino gestured enthusiastically around the Jardin des Tuileries. He was no oil painting, bless him, but at least he was relaxing to look at.

'Remember *Les Nymphéas*,' exclaimed the little teacher, bouncing on his heels with excitement. 'The impact on the eye and the heart! Think of texture and light, of creating your landscape from these. See with Monet's eyes! Use colour! Use emotion!'

'Use a camera, perhaps?' murmured a familiar English voice, carrying in the clear autumn air. 'Technology having advanced since Monet's day.'

Keiko put her sketchbook over her face, snorting with mirth. Signor Poldino reddened, Jake threw Richard a filthy look, but Cormac frowned and called out, 'Give it a rest, Richard.'

'Quite,' snapped Ayeesha. 'Do go on, Signor Poldino. Please. *Some* of us were quite overwhelmed by the waterlilies. Some of us would like to learn more.'

Poldino shot her a grateful look. 'I shall leave you all to wander in the gardens. Please return here in . . .' he checked his old-fashioned pocket watch, '. . . two hours. I am sure *some* of you will produce delightful sketches.' He smiled at Ayeesha and Cormac, then at Cassie.

'God,' Richard murmured to Perry as he stood up and stretched. 'Ayeesha's turning into an insufferable prig. And old Oirish-Eyes is almost as bad.'

Perry sniggered. 'I think he fancies her.'

'Perry!' called Keiko imperiously.

'Go on, you've been summoned. Do try to get some work done too, Peregrine. I don't want my roommate's poor performance reflecting on *me*.'

With another sycophantic chuckle, Perry was gone. Richard was close to Cassie's shoulder, and she felt her heartbeat quicken as he leaned down. 'Come and see my sketchings?' he said seductively.

'Ha ha,' she said, not turning. If he only knew how close he was to a good slap . . . But which of his two faces would she go for? No, better to keep pretending that

119

everything was fine. Cassie wasn't about to have a row with him in front of everybody. He'd caused her enough embarrassment already.

'Sorry. Not funny. Come and be my muse, then, lovely Cassie?'

Cassie concentrated hard on sorting the half-squashed tubes in her paintbox. 'Richard, if it's OK with you, I'd like to . . . um . . . be on my own?' Taking a deep breath, she managed to glance up and force a smile. 'I've never been here before. It's pretty amazing. I need to think about it. If you don't mind.'

'Oh. Of course not.'

His puzzled disappointment sounded genuine. But, then again, so had all his compliments, and Cassie knew now how much they were worth. For a few seconds Richard hovered, as if expecting her to change her mind, then he wandered away.

She breathed out a relieved sigh, and turned. *Damn*. She hadn't thought Ranjit would still be there. He glanced over in her direction, and their eyes met for a split-second, before the unsmiling Indian turned away.

Crossly, Cassie got to her feet and walked swiftly in the opposite direction. There were two hours to kill: surely she could find something paintable, since Poldino obviously expected good work from her again. The gardens were not vast, but she had to avoid Ranjit. And Richard. And Jake, who was in a surly mood. And preferably Keiko too . . . Lordy, her room for manoeuvre was limited.

When she was certain that she was far enough away from everybody else, Cassie sat down on a low wall and began to draw desultory figures in her sketchbook. It was more fun and a lot more involving than she'd expected, but just as her fascination with the tourists was wearing thin, and the crowds were dwindling, she spotted a little girl in a yellow raincoat holding a bright-blue balloon. That was better.

The child noticed the attention, made a face. Cassie made one back. A small tongue came out, and so did Cassie's. Hurriedly sketching the balloon clutched in one fist, Cassie found herself in a face-pulling contest. They were both giggling by the time a parent seized the child's hand and swept her off towards the gallery.

Drat. She hadn't got the collar right: it looked like an Elizabethan ruff. Frustrated, she stared at the gap where the girl had been, and let her eyes wander for the first time in over an hour. They ached from concentrating, so she rubbed them. As her vision cleared, she made out two familiar figures, barely twenty feet away.

Ranjit and Jake.

Ranjit had been sitting on a bench, but he had half-risen to confront Jake, who was standing over him. Jake's posture was aggressive, his expression was twisted with rage, and he was giving Ranjit an earful. Ranjit seemed stunned, as if he'd been caught off guard, and as Jake raised his voice, so did he.

'Jake, would you listen to me, for God's sake—'

Cassie stood up, took a few steps towards them. Both their heads snapped round simultaneously. Without a word, Jake turned and stormed off, his feet crunching on the gravel path. Ranjit sat down heavily.

Cassie hesitated, but something in Ranjit's expression was so miserable she couldn't help herself. She sauntered up to him, trying to look casual.

'What was all that about? Artistic differences?'

With a low groan, he put his face in his hands. Cassie waited, happy to study him. His sleeves were rolled up, revealing golden arms. His hands were beautiful too, and strong, but right now they were white-knuckled and tense.

'Don't want to talk about it, eh?'

'That's right.' He took his hands away from his face and stared after Jake. 'Just like you, Cassandra.'

She shrugged, allowing herself a smile, since he wouldn't see it. His sketchbook was half-open beside him, so she took another sly peek at his face. He still wasn't looking. Leaning down, she flipped the cover back.

If she hadn't gasped, she might have had longer to examine the picture. As it was, he whipped round as fast as a cobra and snatched it away, his dark cheekbones flushed. 'It isn't finished!'

She chewed the corner of her mouth, not quite able to look at him. 'Can I see it when it is?'

'If I ever finish it,' he said curtly as he got to his feet. 'We'd better get back.'

He didn't say another word to her, even though she walked at his side all the way to the Orangerie. They were the last to arrive and Cassie felt several pairs of eyes on them as they arrived. Keiko's glare was ferocious: no doubt it wouldn't be long before Katerina heard how Cassie and Ranjit had emerged from the shrubbery together. Richard's smile was a little less assured than usual; Jake didn't look at anyone or anything.

At least Signor Poldino was delighted to see them. He clapped his chubby hands. 'Wonderful. Now we must return to school, but Cassie, Ranjit! I am looking forward to seeing your finished work.'

I hope Ranjit does finish his, Cassie thought wistfully. And she really hoped he'd let her see it. He'd drawn two simple figures who were watching one another with open delight and amusement: a small girl in a yellow raincoat holding a balloon, and a laughing teenager cross-legged on a low wall, sketching her. The older girl looked so carefree, it would have been easy not to recognise herself.

She did, though.

*

'Ooh, pretty woman,' sang an American voice.

Cassie snapped her head up, expecting to see Jake's familiar features.

But it was Richard. He dumped his books on Jake's desk, pulled out his chair and slumped down, linking his hands behind his head in a fair imitation of the American's cocky attitude.

Cassie scrutinised him. 'You're good at that.'

'What?'

'Mimicking. You sounded just like him.'

'Why, thank you.' He batted his long lashes at her.

'Pretty good actor all round, really.'

'Hm?' His body tensed, very slightly.

It put her in mind of a snake, somehow. Like the way a snake's whole length tightened like a spring, just before it struck out. *Be careful*, Jake had said in the restaurant. Falling out with Richard could be really, really stupid, for more than one reason.

Not that she was taking Jake's advice. But she wouldn't find out the Academy's secrets by having a strop with anyone who hacked her off. So don't get mad, she told herself: get even.

Besides, Richard wasn't the only decent actor around here. Cassie gave him a grin that put the big, easy smile back on his face. 'Where's Jake?'

'He's not coming to classes today.' Richard's shoulders lifted slightly. 'He isn't too well, I heard. Suffers from insomnia, you know. Perhaps he had a particularly bad night.'

'Shame,' said Cassie lightly. 'So. You been avoiding me or something?'

'Darling!' He sat a little straighter. 'I thought *you'd* been avoiding *me!*'

'Course not. I've been busy, that's all.'

'And a bit sleepless yourself. I nearly fell off my chair when I saw you at the common-room door the other night.' He was all concern, leaning forward. 'Listen, if you want to see the place that much, I can try and arrange something.'

She gave him a sheepish grin. 'Actually, I'd really like that. I got a bit lost, that's all. I like walking round at night when I can't sleep. I always did. Better than just lying there, staring at the ceiling.'

125

'Thinking of England,' drawled Richard. 'I do like the image you conjure up.'

Cassie laughed. 'I'll say it again. You're the *limit*, you.'

From the front of the classroom there was a cough. 'Victor Hugo, ladies and gentlemen. Would you please turn to page fourteen . . .'

Madame Lefèvre wasn't exactly the hardest disciplinarian in the school, and she was short-sighted into the bargain. Cassie could sense Richard fidgeting and flicking ahead through the pages. At last he leaned across.

'You're interested in the Few, aren't you?' he whispered.

Cassie tapped her open book with a forefinger, feigning disapproval. He sat back and sighed. In less than a minute, though, he was leaning towards her again. 'Look, I can tell you what happens. I've seen the movie.'

'There's a movie?' she whispered. 'About the Few?'

He grinned. 'Tease. I mean The Hunchback. He dies, OK? I'm bored. So how interested are you?'

'Get over yourself. And shush.'

He muffled a laugh. 'In the Few, I mean. How interested? Would you like to be a member?'

Cassie blinked, rendered speechless. This she hadn't expected. Low sun streamed through the tall windows, making it hard to see Richard's face, but there was something eager in his voice.

'Are you serious?'

'Mademoiselle BELL!'

'Sorry.'

Cassie tried to take in the page in front of her, but her concentration was shattered. To be a member of the Few! What better way to find out what was going on here? Surreptitiously she turned again to Richard. She'd caught him unawares, and his stare was different, more intent. Embarrassed, he faked a grin and returned to his book.

Aha! He did like her after all, she realised with amusement. She wasn't going to be taken in by him again, but he actually *did* like her. He'd been acting the bitch with Katerina that day, just as he'd acted the lovestruck swain with Cassie. But he didn't know Cassie had overheard him. That gave her the advantage. It was pretty obvious he didn't want to offend Katerina – but he didn't want to fall out with Cassie either. Oh, this could get interesting. She smothered a smile.

What a lot of masks he wore. Maybe even Richard didn't know any more which was the real one. Still, there was nothing sinister about a bit of playacting. He was looking out for himself, and Cassie had to admit that appealed to her. She knew how to watch out for herself, too. She could understand the instinct.

Be careful, Cassie. Hearing Jake's voice again in her

head, she frowned. What had happened to Jake, anyway? Too much night prowling, as Richard had hinted?

He wasn't the only one throwing a sickie, either. Alice wasn't at her desk.

'You'd be great for the Few,' Richard murmured. 'Some of them really like you. They think you have . . . spirit.'

'Oh, yeah?' Cassie remembered the empty desk three rows in front. 'What's happened to Alice?'

'Oh, Alice.' There was a grin in his low voice. 'Still getting over her hangover, I should think.'

'From three nights ago?' Cassie raised her eyebrows.

'Well. That girl can knock 'em back, let me tell you. And of course she was a little over-excited about being invited to the common room. You'd never be that silly, would you?'

Cassie frowned. Over-excited? That wasn't what she'd call it. That wasn't how Alice had looked, perched on that chair with the silver cup clutched in her hands, skin pale, eyes dull, body limp.

'No,' she murmured at last, managing a dry laugh. 'I'm not that easily impressed, sunshine.'

'I know.' He winked. 'That's why you'd be ideal. And someone already recommended you.'

Cassie stared. 'Who? Sir Alric?'

'God, no.' Richard looked alarmed. 'Don't tell him we

had this conversation, will you? I'm not supposed to – um – speak out of turn. Keep it secret for now, OK?'

'I'm hardly likely to be having a cosy chat with him.' Cassie's tone turned frosty. Why would Sir Alric object to her? Obviously Richard was still a crashing snob, if he couldn't own up to liking her. Once more she was unsure if she liked and trusted Richard, or couldn't stand him. 'So who, then? Who recommended me?'

'Someone very important. That's all you—'

'Monsieur Halton-Jones! Perhaps you would like to give us your insights into the structure of these opening chapters?'

'Madame Lefèvre, of course!' Richard threw the teacher a dazzling smile and cleared his throat, flipping open his notebook.

She'd probably imagined it, thought Cassie: the nervous relief on Madame's face. A little flushed, as if she'd got away with heinous cheek by daring to scold a member of the Few. A pulse throbbing fast in her temple.

Richard stretched out his long legs and crossed them at the ankles. 'Poor Quasimodo,' he began. 'The tragedy is foreshadowed from the outset . . .'

CHAPTER ELEVEN

There was too much on Cassie's mind. Her thoughts and suspicions were chaotic, and she knew no more about Victor Hugo than she had an hour ago. At this rate she'd be expelled for incompetence before she discovered a thing. Students pushed past her in the corridor, rushing to their next class, but Cassie found she had to walk slowly, thinking furiously, examining her options.

Richard wouldn't have mentioned the possibility of her becoming one of the Few if he didn't mean it seriously; she was sure of that. Thinking of Isabella, her conscience twanged painfully. If Cassie was invited to join the Few, would her roommate be terribly hurt? Should she confide in Isabella, or leave her in blissful, safe ignorance? And how risky was it to let herself be recruited? Distracted, Cassie barely knew where she was, let alone which class she was heading for.

Which was why she nearly jumped out of her skin when the door opened at her side.

She came to a dead halt, heart thumping.

'Cassie! I hoped I'd catch you.'

The mellifluous voice was instantly recognisable, as were the height and the presence. Just as well, since she was so close she was gaping only at his blazer buttons and his chic silk tie.

'Hello, Sir Alric.' She blinked up into the starkly handsome face.

'Lost again?' he asked mischievously.

She shook her head. Beyond him she glimpsed his office. Dark-green curtains were swagged back with gold cords. A vast mahogany desk took up most of one wall, beyond an expanse of thick carpet. In the middle of the room was a smaller table, Sèvres porcelain cups and a silver teapot perched on top; two pale-yellow armchairs huddled close around it like old friends. In one of them sat a recognisable figure who laughed lightly and clapped her frail hands together.

'Cassandra, my dear.' Estelle Azzedine didn't try to stand. 'How lovely! Are you enjoying the Academy?'

'Great. Fine. I mean, I love it.' Cassie smiled awkwardly back. 'Hello, Madame Azzedine.'

'Estelle.' Wagging a finger, Madame Azzedine gave her

a playful frown.

Sir Alric looked from one to the other. 'You've met?'

'On Cassandra's very first day. She was kind enough to help me up the steps.'

He gave the old woman an amused smile. 'Did she, indeed? And speaking of your first day, Cassie, when we finally met this week I was reminded of how long you had been at the Academy before I introduced myself. Allow me to make up for my bad manners. Do join us for tea.'

Nervously she checked her watch. 'But I've got—'

'A class with Mr Chelnikov? Don't worry about that. Marat!'

Cassie almost leaped sideways. The squat porter had appeared silently at her back. He wore a baleful expression on his stony face.

'Marat. Please inform Gospodin Chelnikov that Miss Bell is excused his class for today. I wish to speak to her. Apologise to him on my behalf.'

Marat nodded once, silent, and turned away.

'Come in, Cassie.' Sir Alric closed the heavy door and pulled up another chair opposite Madame Azzedine, who winked at Cassie.

'What a lovely treat for me. Young company. Are you making the most of the school's opportunities as I recommended, Cassandra?'

'Yes. I mean . . .' With a pang of guilt, Cassie remembered the last wasted hour. 'I'm trying.' She shrugged ruefully.

'And succeeding very well. Cassie is extremely able in a wide range of subjects.' Sir Alric gave her an approving glance. 'I think I can safely say she is one of the most deserving scholarship students we have ever had.'

'How marvellous!' Madame Azzedine sat a little straighter. 'Intelligent, then?'

'Yes, indeed,' said Sir Alric, pouring tea steadily into a delicate cup for Cassie.

'And very pretty, too! What striking looks you have, my dear. I have never seen eyes of such an unusual colour. Don't you think so, Sir Alric?'

'I hadn't thought about it.' He smiled at Cassie, almost complicitly. 'I dare say you're right. Cassie, what I really wanted to talk about was the other night. It worries me that you don't sleep well. And I hope what you saw didn't . . . upset you. I meant what I said about coming to me with any problems.'

'Oh, don't worry,' she said cheerfully, pleased they'd finished with the subject of her looks. 'I never did sleep well. And there were a lot more problems at Cranlake Crescent.'

'Ah. Of course. I expect life didn't always go smoothly there.' He looked at her kindly.

Just as she decided she really liked him, Madame Azzedine butted in again. 'Tell me about this, Cassandra. You have had a difficult life, yes?'

Taken aback, Cassie paused for a sip of tea. It had a perfumed taste that she didn't much like, but it gave her a moment to think. 'I . . . suppose so. I dunno. I did have a few foster families. Not many, though.' She grinned suddenly. 'Bit disruptive, I suppose. Hard to handle. I always ended up back at Cranlake Crescent.'

Nobody wants you, you little waste of space. Nobody!

'Hard to handle!' Interrupting Jilly's voice in her head, Madame Azzedine gave a throaty laugh. 'That simply means you have spirit, my dear. And to do so well in your studies despite all the difficulties – well, how marvellous. We are lucky to have Cassandra here. Are we not, Sir Alric?'

'Indeed.' He shifted his position between Cassie and Madame Azzedine, slightly blocking the old woman's intent gaze. Cassie blushed furiously, uncomfortable with the torrent of compliments. Still, she appreciated Madame Azzedine being so nice to her. Sir Alric didn't have to look quite so disapproving.

She put down her cup quickly. 'I'd better go.'

Sir Alric checked his wristwatch. 'Yes. Perhaps you had better.'

They were both watching her, only one of them smiling, as the door swung softly closed once more.

'Cassie! Cassie, look at this!'

Isabella's miserable mood of the last forty-eight hours had evaporated. Damn, thought Cassie as she hesitated in the doorway of their room.

'See what he has given me!'

Flaming Nora. She had no idea that orchids grew so big. Was it genetically modified or what? Pure white and very beautiful, it must have cost Jake a lot more than he could afford. This might have been one of Cassie's less-smart ideas; after all, she didn't want Isabella getting her hopes up. At least Jake had been true to his word, though.

'You know, there's something about orchids I don't like.' Cassie wrinkled her nose. 'Those black ones in the courtyard by the statue? They're sinister.'

'Oh, those are Sir Alric's favourites. The signature flower of the Academy, but no one else has ever seen or heard of them. I've asked. Even Mama does not know them, and she is something of an expert.'

'Really?' Cassie suddenly felt uneasy.

'Ah, but this orchid!' Isabella laughed, not in the least put out, and ran her finger across one pristine petal. 'Pure, but sexy. And so romantic!'

Cassie had to smile. 'OK. It's gorgeous.'

'Just like Jake, hm?' Isabella planted a delicate kiss on the flower. 'And there is something for you too, Cassie.'

'From Jake?' asked Cassie, surprised.

Isabella shrugged, still smiling idiotically at her orchid. 'I don't know. I don't think so, it is not his handwriting. Here.'

She tossed an envelope at Cassie, who snatched it from the air. She recognised that rich, parchment-like paper. Academy paper. Oh, hell; had Sir Alric found her tea-time manners lacking? Was this her kiss-off letter?

With one trembling finger she slit the flap and pulled out an embossed card. Cassie had to read it over three times before she could bring herself to meet Isabella's curious gaze.

'Isabella.' She bit her lip.

'What? What is it?'

'I so hope you really don't care about this. I don't want to spoil your evening.' Swallowing, Cassie turned the card towards her friend, and watched Isabella's smile die as she read:

The Darke Academy

From the Office of the Few

*Your name has been submitted to the Congress
as a potential candidate for membership of the Few.
Please attend at the Common Room of the Few
on November 12th, at 7.00 pm.
Punctuality is expected.*

CHAPTER TWELVE

'Gentlemen. Ready?'

Both boys nodded, saluted Señor Alvarez and each other, and slipped their fencing masks over their faces.

'*En garde*, then. Ready? *Fence.*'

As Richard lunged hard at Ranjit, and Ranjit took a step back, parried and riposted, Cassie fiddled uneasily with her body wire. She'd already made a pig's ear of getting her kit on and she was never going to look as elegant as Ranjit or Richard. Or any of them, for that matter. Isabella, in fencing whites and with a glossy ponytail tumbling down her back, looked like a martial goddess. She rested her fingertips casually on her *épée*, mask tucked under one arm, as she chatted to Perry, whom she'd just comprehensively thrashed.

Guilt nagged at Cassie. Isabella was trying hard to act normal, but her couldn't-care-less attitude to Cassie's news didn't ring quite true. When she sat down at last, pushing back damp strands of mahogany hair, Cassie smiled at her. Maybe she was doing too much smiling herself lately, and maybe that wasn't very normal either.

Cassie took a breath. 'Isabella.' She paused. 'Do you mind about me getting an interview?'

The interview was tomorrow. The thought of it had already been keeping her awake, and now a small thrill rippled down her vertebrae.

For once Isabella didn't protest or shrug the question off with a laugh. Seriously she studied Cassie's face.

'Truly, I don't mind. You deserve it, you—' Isabella paused. 'Perhaps I'm just disappointed. That again they have not asked me. But I'm happy for you. Yes?' Her smile seemed taut.

'It should have been you. I'm sorry. I'm new, and you've got more right to it, and—'

'No, it isn't that. It's just . . .' Reddening, Isabella clamped her mouth shut.

'What?' Cassie frowned.

'Nothing.'

'It's not nothing. Tell me.' Cassie's tone had a dangerous edge. 'Give, Isabella.'

'Look, it's not what *I* think. People are taken aback, that's all. Because . . .'

139

Cassie waited.

Her roommate's words came out in a rush. 'A scholarship student has never been asked before. That's all.'

'I see.' Cassie tugged off her fencing glove and twisted it.

Isabella pulled her hair free from its ponytail. 'Cassie, I don't think it's – *wrong*, or anything. It just goes to show how special you are, yes? It's just that some in the school are . . .'

'Surprised,' said Cassie, 'Yeah. And I'm guessing it's not in a nice way.'

Isabella opened her mouth to answer, but an electronic beep signalled another hit and Cassie turned her attention back to the *piste*. Ranjit, unflustered, had scored off Richard. Again.

Mean and magnificent, faces obscured by black mesh, jackets and breeches tight over muscles . . . It was enough to make a girl light-headed. You could never mistake one for the other, though, even when their faces were covered. Both were fast and light-footed, and both made their strikes like cunning snakes, but one of them was just insanely elegant, every movement economical, graceful and woundingly effective.

Boy, did Ranjit look good with a weapon.

'Cassie!'

She blinked, stunned, and Isabella nudged her hard. 'Eyes front,' her roommate whispered mischievously, all her good humour restored. 'You're on.'

The bout was over; Richard and Ranjit had tugged off their masks and were shaking hands. Fifteen-nine, she noted, glancing at the score. To Ranjit, of course.

She tried to be disappointed.

'Cassie,' said Señor Alvarez again. 'On *piste*, please. One of you two, stay.'

'I'll fence her,' offered Richard eagerly.

'No.' Ranjit stepped in front of him. 'I will.'

Richard seemed about to argue, then he shrugged and unplugged his body wire, offering the connection to Cassie.

'Damn,' she muttered. 'He'll hammer me.'

'Huh,' whispered Richard, offended. 'You don't think I would?'

'Yeah, OK,' she grinned as he clipped her wire on to the back of her jacket, turned her by one shoulder and closed her Velcro neck fastening. Richard was so close she could feel his warm breath, smell his fresh sweat; his fingers were almost brushing her throat. She could feel disapproval, too, radiating from the silent Ranjit like a physical force.

Ranjit didn't smile as he saluted, then pulled his black mask over his face.

'Remember, Cassie,' said Señor Alvarez beside her, 'keep your wrist *so*, your body angled *so*. You are still giving your opponent too many chances, you are vulnerable to hits. And do not back off all the time! Do not be afraid to lunge. Now! Ready?'

Nod, salute, mask on.

'*En garde*. Ready? *Fence.*'

It was hopeless. Ranjit got past every parry with no effort, blocked every thrust she made. The electronic counter sounded with embarrassing regularity, and Cassie almost fainted with relief when Ranjit made one mistake and she made a hit by default. At least he wouldn't be wiping the floor with her, fifteen-nil.

Cassie was well aware of Katerina, her own bout over, watching and smirking, and when Ranjit stepped back and removed his mask, then extended his gloved fingers for a curt handshake, Cassie felt only overwhelmingly glad that it was over.

'Fifteen-one, on my right.' Señor Alvarez sounded disappointed, but not remotely surprised. 'Isabella. Richard. On *piste* please.'

As Cassie disconnected her body wire and offered him the connection, Richard's fingers brushed hers.

'Pretty unchivalrous,' he murmured. 'I'd have let you make a few hits.'

'What would be the point of that?' asked Ranjit contemptuously as he swept past towards the bench.

When he was gone, Cassie winked at Richard. 'He's right, of course.'

'Albeit an almighty pain in the arse.'

'Good luck.' She smiled as Richard turned to salute Isabella.

Ranjit sat alone on the bench, a six-foot gap between him and a Year Ten called Hamid, who despite being one of the Few himself, eyed Ranjit with something close to nervousness. Well, Cassie wasn't scared of him.

Not off-*piste*, anyway . . .

Cassie slumped down at Ranjit's side, tossing her mask lightly up and down.

'Would you mind not doing that? It's very irritating.'

Sighing, Cassie put her mask on her lap. Katerina was looking daggers at her from her place by the water cooler, but the fast ring of clashing blades and the constant buzzing of the monitor meant she wouldn't hear anything Cassie said to Ranjit.

'I'll get a proper hit on you one day, mate,' she told him cheerfully.

'I dare say you will. But not because I let you.' He gave

Richard, who was backing away from Isabella's thrust, a look of disdain.

And he had the nerve to say *she* was irritating? Cassie turned angrily. 'You don't like me, do you?'

'It's nothing to do with that.'

'What's it to do with then? Educational funding?'

'That's beneath you.'

'Funny. I thought it was beneath *you*.'

'Cassandra.' He took a breath. 'Stop trying to make me dislike you.'

She shrugged. 'I don't think I have to try, do I?'

'I told you, it's got nothing to do with disliking you.'

'You haven't told me what it *is* to do with, have you?'

He tugged savagely at the Velcro fastening on his mask, so that it made a loud ripping noise. He refastened it, and did it again. Señor Alvarez, standing close by, grimaced, so Ranjit stopped playing with the Velcro and looked hard at Cassie.

'I don't like how you make me feel. *OK?*'

'Oh.' That took the wind out of her sails.

'I can't possibly be involved with someone like you.'

Anger sparked again, quick and fierce. The *jerk*. 'Oh, likewise.' She stood up.

Ranjit bit his lip. 'I didn't mean—'

'Yeah, I think you did.'

Seizing her wrist, he pulled, and she sank back quickly into her place on the bench. He was incredibly strong.

'I didn't mean it like that, I swear.' Letting her go, he drew a hand across his face. 'I mean, the way you make me feel – and you do – well, I can't accept it, Cassandra.'

'Can't *accept* it?'

'That's right.' Suddenly and without warning, he stretched out and stroked her hair very gently. The featherlight sensation made her shiver.

'Meaning?' Pulling away, she folded her arms.

'Meaning what I say.' Irritation crept back into his voice. 'I always do.'

Cassie felt a glare: Katerina, incandescent with rage.

'Looks like class is over,' she said abruptly, standing up again. 'And I'll spontaneously combust if I don't get out of somebody's line of sight.'

Glancing past her, Ranjit's expression hardened as he caught sight of the glowering Swede.

What was it with him? He grated on her nerves like fingernails down a blackboard, but she still found herself seeking out his company. She didn't even mind a fifteen-to-one thrashing, if it was at his hands.

Giving herself a mental slap, she went over to where Richard and Isabella were packing up their weapons and body wires. Richard was dripping with sweat.

'She beat me,' he told Cassie ruefully.

'Naturally,' smirked Isabella.

'I'm never fencing you again when I'm this tired. Chuck me that towel, will you?'

As Isabella turned to reach for it, Richard shrugged off his fencing jacket and plastron. Under it, he was wearing only a sleeveless vest that hugged his muscles tightly. Vain devil, thought Cassie, amused. He knew very well he looked darn good in defeat.

As she wound her own body wire into a loop, her brow furrowed. There was a nasty-looking scar on Richard's shoulder blade. When she looked closer, though, she could see the mark was a clear pattern of intertwining lines, about two inches in diameter. It was permanent, like a brand, and she'd never seen anything quite like it.

Richard smiled at her over his shoulder, but as he caught her eye his grin died and he hurriedly snatched up a sweatshirt and pulled it on. That was no act, Cassie decided. That had been a real mistake. And the way Ranjit was glowering at Richard, he thought so too.

'Hey!' Isabella nudged her hard again and thrust a towel into her hands. 'Can you stop ogling Richard's sweating flanks for a second? Let's go shower, you wicked, wicked girl. Before you see something you are not supposed to!'

Cassie tried to catch Richard's eye as Isabella tugged her out of the sports hall, but he had turned away.

'Isabella,' she murmured under her breath, 'I think I already did.'

CHAPTER THIRTEEN

'Richard, darling. Thank you for bringing the candidate.'

Katerina sat in a gilt chair, ankles elegantly crossed. She didn't so much as glance at Cassie, but every other person in the room did. Cassie could feel the impact of their collective stare like a physical force. If it hadn't been for Richard's firm hand in the small of her back, she might have turned on her heel and left.

'You'll be fine, he murmured; then, out loud, 'I think most of us know Cassie, don't we? Except perhaps you guys.' Richard gestured towards three tall, beautiful sixth formers, who Cassie had seen from a distance. 'Vassily, India, Sara, this is Cassie Bell. She joined the Academy this term.'

'Oh, everyone knows Cassie.' Katerina poured herself a glass of red wine, exchanging a sly smirk with Keiko. 'It feels as if she has always been with us.'

'Come along and sit down, now, Cassie.' Cormac Doyle gestured to a chair in the centre of their group, giving her a wink and an enchanting grin. 'Katerina can be intimidating, but nobody else bites.'

Richard jiggled the chair encouragingly.

'Yes,' added Ayeesha. 'Tell us about yourself, Cassie. That's why you're here.' Her smile was radiant.

Uncertainly Cassie sat down, half-expecting a whoopee cushion. No such childish tricks, though. They sat in a semicircle around her, some lounging, some sitting elegantly upright, but everyone intent and watchful. No Ranjit, she couldn't help noticing. Again.

'Will Ranjit be joining us?' asked Cormac, as if reading her mind.

'No,' said Katerina quickly. She sounded tense, but almost relieved. 'Mikhail, if you feel quite up to it, perhaps we might begin.'

'I'm fine,' said a hoarse voice from the edge of the semicircle. 'Go ahead.'

Cassie turned to look. The Year Ten boy with the shaggy blond hair had bone structure almost as beautiful as Katerina's, but it was way too prominent. His face was gaunt and drawn, his skin pale and dry like paper. A water bottle sat on the floor beside his chair, but when he lifted it to his mouth, it was empty. Katerina gave an exasperated sigh whilst Ayeesha got up and brought him another. Gratefully he seized it and swigged thirstily.

'Still got that nasty bug?' asked Richard smoothly. 'Bad luck, Mikhail. Now, I've been asked to propose Cassie. What can I say? She's clever, she's tough, she's been brought up the hard way – unlike most of us – and she's quite strikingly pretty.'

'Hmph,' muttered Keiko. Katerina only raised her fingers to her mouth, not quite hiding a superior smile.

'And,' continued Richard, unperturbed, 'let me emphasise it again: she has caught the eye of a highly respected member of the Few. We all know how much weight this particular opinion carries, so I believe that's all I need to say. Any questions?'

'Well, Richard,' said Mikhail after a brief silence. 'Nobody could ever accuse you of ranting on at length.' Clearing his throat harshly, he took another long pull at his water.

'Cassie.' Ayeesha leaned forward a little, and Cassie smiled in relief. She at least was friendly. 'What brought you to the Darke Academy?'

She didn't hesitate. 'A scholarship.'

Ayeesha nodded, but a snigger erupted from Keiko. With an effort of will Cassie managed not to rise to the bait.

'Of course, we knew that,' said Ayeesha. She seemed pleased with Cassie's blunt response. 'Good for you.' She raised a warning finger at the others. 'It does present a slight problem. A technicality, really.'

'Not at all. A scholarship', said Cormac, 'means Sir Alric brought her here. He checks over the exam results and the interview transcripts. Well, now, could there be any higher recommendation?' He surveyed the semicircle, smiling.

'The Few have never accepted a scholarship student.' Keiko, of course. Her arms were tightly folded, her lips pursed. 'I've never heard anything like it.'

'Now,' murmured Katerina. 'I must admit it would be *quite* a break with tradition. But there's a first time for everything, Keiko.'

Cassie clamped her lips together, more to stop herself laughing than snapping back. Katerina and Keiko were being ridiculously pompous, and some of the other Few members obviously thought so too. India mimed a yawn behind Katerina's back. Ayeesha nudged Cormac, almost giggling. Richard, flopping on to a sofa, gave her a wink.

Katerina ignored them. 'Why don't you tell us a little about your family?'

'Because she doesn't have one,' snapped Keiko, red with humiliation.

151

Cool, Cassie. Stay cool. 'My dad's out of the picture,' she said crisply, 'but like the rest of you, I had one.'

'And your mother shunted you into care, presumably. Were you a little inconvenient?'

'She makes a habit of it,' growled Keiko.

'Or perhaps,' continued Katerina, 'you just weren't worth the effort.'

The misery was so hot and so sudden Cassie had to draw breath. And it still hurt. Like Jilly Beaton all over again, making her believe it. *Not worth the effort, slut.*

Richard was watching her steadily.

Cassie smiled, broadly and insincerely. 'My mother couldn't handle me.'

Richard gave an appreciative nod. 'Who could?'

'Quite,' said Cassie curtly. 'Her new guy didn't want me around. She wanted him more than she wanted me, and anyway, they've got a replacement now. A boy. Frankly, I'm glad I'm out of it. I'm no more interested in them than they are in me. Next question?'

She'd silenced them, she thought with fierce satisfaction. Just for a moment, she'd shut up the smug gits.

In the silence, someone cleared his throat and said hoarsely, 'Can we consider the school's rationale?'

Mikhail again. His attention was riveted on Cassie as he

fumbled for his water bottle once more. Some of the liquid trickled from the side of his mouth, and he had to wipe his chin with the back of one shaking hand. If anything he looked worse than before, but no one seemed very concerned. Cassie frowned.

'There was a time,' he went on, his voice almost reduced to a whisper, 'when scholarship students had a more useful function than . . . public relations.'

Cassie's sympathy melted, replaced by unease. Function? Keiko's words in the hall came back to her: *You're here for our benefit, not the other way round.*

'Mikhail.' That was a sixth-form chess prodigy called Yusuf. He stood in shadow, and Cassie hadn't noticed him till he spoke. 'You have not been one of us for very long. You're new and inexperienced. Don't pretend to know as much as we do.'

'It's part of the Few history. I've been reading up on it.' Mikhail had linked his fingers together, so tightly his knuckles were bone-white. His body was hunched, coiled like a spring, but he seemed unable to stop looking at Cassie.

OK. What she ought to do was get up and walk out. It would be a retreat she'd never live down, but what the heck. She didn't even like the common room, now she was in it. The furnishings were all so dark. Chairs, curtains, wallpaper, silk lampshades: all the fabrics were ruby and purple and deep-water-green. The room was warm with colour, but somehow menacing too. It was beautiful – everywhere in this place was beautiful – but the air was oppressive. She didn't want to be in here. Not now, not ever.

No. She wasn't going to walk out. This was her chance to find out the secrets of the Few, but that wasn't all. She was as good as this lot. Better. She wasn't going to tug her forelock and scurry away like a scared mouse. Tightening her jaw, she looked across at Keiko, studying the girl as minutely and disdainfully as Keiko was inspecting her.

That crisp white shirt she was wearing, a stunning contrast to her blue-black hair: it was Chanel wasn't it? Of course, for all Cassie knew it could be George At Asda – except that she recognised it as one Isabella had rejected only last week. Better not mention that to Keiko, then. Cassie's rigid smile relaxed into a genuine, broad grin. She felt a lot better already.

'Traditions change.' Richard was beaming at her. He looked pleased and proud. 'They evolve. Everything evolves. Even us.' He gave a gurgling laugh.

'I'm so thirsty,' moaned Mikhail softly.

'Look,' said Cassie, glancing anxiously around the

remaining Few and then back at Mikhail, 'I know it's none of my business, but are you all right?'

'Fine,' snapped Mikhail, febrile eyes burning.

'Oh, for heaven's sake.' Katerina snapped her fingers. At the back of the room, Hamid rose with a weary sigh and replaced the empty water bottle with a full one once more.

Cassie stared. 'Look. He isn't well.'

'Now, that really *is* none of your business.' Katerina gave her a tight formal smile. 'Not until you are one of us.'

The sixth former Sara leaned forward, smiling intently. 'And I think you have a really good chance of that, Cassie. I'm sure we can overcome . . . objections. She is very pretty, I think.' She addressed that remark to the room in general, obviously not expecting an answer. 'The Elders like that in a candidate.'

What has that got to do with anything, you crowd of shallow freaks? Cassie managed to bite back the question as Richard's hand touched her shoulder lightly.

'Pretty?' mused Katerina. 'I suppose so. She has unusual looks. True beauty, I think, requires a touch of cruelty. That seems to be missing.'

'Good,' muttered Cassie under her breath.

Richard shot her a warning look.

'With the right . . . guidance, I think she could be

lovely.' Sara smiled again. Cassie was beginning to dislike those smiles. 'Don't you agree?'

Get me out of here! These Few weren't just shallow, they were sinister. Maybe it was time to leave after all.

Richard clapped his hands together. 'Anybody have any more questions?'

'The most important one.' Mikhail's voice was faint. 'The one we agreed was necessary.'

'Of course.' Katerina turned her glass in her fingers, watching the red wine swirl. 'There is only one vacancy, and it is *hotly* desired by several students.'

'Perry Hutton, for one,' snapped Keiko. It was obvious who she wanted.

'And Isabella Caruso,' lilted Katerina. 'Bella, bella Isabella.'

Yusuf's voice was a hypnotic murmur. 'So our question is . . .'

'How would you feel . . .' said Vassily.

'About denying your dearest friend . . .' said Sara.

Katerina's lips curved in a gleaming smile: '. . . her heart's desire.'

Silence fell as they watched her.

Cassie swallowed. Impeccable Katerina Svensson, she noticed with amusement, had tiny red wine stains in the creases of her lips. She wasn't afraid of them, but they were right. What she *was* afraid of was hurting Isabella. What a clever question, and on it might hinge her future with the Few.

Did she want it that much? Even to discover the dark heart of the Academy? Did she want it enough to sacrifice Isabella's friendship?

'Thirsty,' rasped Mikhail.

His throat jerked as he gulped down water. The others were treating him with mild pity, but little concern. What was their problem? Wasn't he pretty enough when he was sick? Isabella was more beautiful than any of them, and cruelty didn't come into it. Her beauty wasn't all in her epidermis.

'Well?' snapped Katerina. 'We're waiting. Do you care about hurting your best friend? To the bone?'

The answer came to her suddenly, and it seemed blindingly obvious.

'No.' Cassie met each hard stare in turn. 'No. Why would I?'

Vassily persisted. 'Because she *is* your best friend, and you're famously close? Just a notion we thought you might want to consider,' he added sarcastically.

'You're a spoilt bunch of brats.'

'Hey,' interrupted Cormac, 'who are you calling spoilt?'

Cassie ignored him. 'You don't know what it means to

be at this school. I wouldn't expect you to understand. You've never known anything but privilege, have you? You've never been miserable or helpless.'

They had all stiffened. Even Ayeesha's welcoming smile had faded. Mikhail looked as if he was about to get to his feet and come towards her, but Katerina had lifted a warning hand, and for now he was gripping the arms of his chair and staying where he was. The older ones – Sara, Vassily, Yusuf – had a strange look. Amusement? Curiosity?

Now, thought Cassie. Now was her chance to tell this lot what she thought of them and get out of here. What was she doing with these people? *You so do not want to be here, Cassie . . .*

No. Inwardly she gave herself a kick. She knew very well what she was doing here, after all. The more she saw of this gang, the more she wanted to know. *Knowledge is power, Cassie.* And a little power might be something she was going to need around here, if she wasn't going to go under.

She took a shaking breath. 'The Darke Academy is my chance to make something of myself. If I was a member of the Few as well? I'd never be miserable or powerless or poor again, would I? I'm sick of all that. Sick of it.'

'How sick, exactly?' Vassily asked smoothly.

'I'm not fool enough to think you all like me,' said Cassie, keeping her voice level, 'but you're contacts. You're kind of a network, aren't you? Isn't that what the Few are all about?'

The remaining Few looked at one another. Some of them smiled.

Mustn't blow it, thought Cassie. *Not now*.

'So I might lose a friend. So what? I can make more. Sure, I like Isabella. But she's not . . .' Hardening her heart, she took a breath. 'She's not indispensable.'

The silence was even heavier. Richard looked expressionless, Sara amused, Ayeesha a little disappointed. Katerina had a surprisingly satisfied air.

Vassily leaned back in his chair and stretched. 'Well, I think Cassie has dealt with our main concern admirably. Thank you Cassie. Everyone, it's getting on. Do we all agree that we have enough to let the proposal go forward?' The sixth former scanned the room quizzically.

'Absolutely,' said Ayeesha, checking her watch. 'I agree, and I see no need to drag this out. I told Freya I'd meet her in the library in a quarter of an hour, and I don't want to let her down.'

'Quite,' muttered Vassily, rather bitchily. 'After all, she never lets *you* down.'

Cormac shot him a dirty look. 'Come on, Ayeesha.' He

stood up. 'Let's not waste more time. Cassie, that was a very interesting interview. Very interesting. I had you down as somebody else.'

'Me too.' Ayeesha was smiling again, but a bit more warily. Then she took Cormac's hand and they left.

Much to Cassie's discomfort, a few others did, too, India among them. There wasn't a sympathetic face left. Except for Richard, of course.

'Well,' she said brightly. 'I suppose I should go too. Thanks for inviting me. It's been—'

'Stay a bit longer,' murmured Richard, pressing her back into her seat. 'I thought you wanted to see the common room?'

'I did, but . . .' She glanced a little desperately at the door, just closing behind a Year Ten girl she vaguely knew and liked.

'Go on, I'll show you the Matisse. It's incredible.'

'Maybe another time.'

Too late. The door clicked shut, and intense silence fell on the room. Cassie tried to catch Richard's eye, but he wasn't paying attention. She fidgeted, wondered if she should just get up and leave.

But then Mikhail stood abruptly, knocking over his water bottle, and took a step towards her. Cassie no longer felt fidgety; now she was frightened.

'I don't feel well.'

Hamid half-rose. 'Katerina, stop him!'

Katerina snapped, 'Mikhail!'

He stopped, wobbling.

'Go back to your room. You're not fit to be here. Your roommate must be back from his parents' by now. He can . . . look after you.'

'Oh, Katerina, let him have a drink.' Keiko batted her lashes. 'A *proper* drink. And why don't we offer Cassie one, while we're at it?'

'Well,' said Yusuf, watching Mikhail, whose chest was rising and falling hard. 'Where's the harm in it?'

Shocked, Hamid turned. 'Yusuf! You know what *he* said.'

'Ooh, Hamid!' scoffed Keiko. 'You might be afraid of Ranjit, but Katerina isn't.'

'Indeed I'm not,' snapped Katerina. 'But there are certain wishes we must respect.'

'I thought that's what we were trying to do. More's the pity.'

'Opinions vary, Keiko. Opinions vary.'

'Someone . . . offer our guest . . . a drink. *Please*.'

'Mikhail, you're becoming delirious. What a greenhorn you are. Next time we expect you to plan ahead a little better! Hamid, take him to his room.'

'But, Katerina . . .' whinged Mikhail.

'To be honest,' shrugged Vassily, 'I'm with Keiko and Yusuf. It's not as if we can't still consider her afterwards. It's only one drink.'

Sara chuckled. 'Hamid, Katerina, lighten up! Now, Cassie, we've been inhospitable. Will you drink with us?' Rising, she turned to a tray on the gloomy sideboard.

Cassie watched the statuesque beauty, feeling terribly uneasy. It didn't seem right or even possible to jump up and leave. That would be running away. But she *so* did *not* want a drink . . .

'After all,' drawled Keiko, 'Ranjit isn't here. He can't care so terribly much.'

'I thought you'd had a final warning, Keiko?' Vassily seemed entertained by her rebelliousness.

Keiko preened. 'Yes, but Sir Alric's not here either, is he?'

'Oh, have it your way,' snapped Katerina. 'Make it quick, Mikhail!'

Blissfully Mikhail sighed, all the tension draining from his body. He stalked towards Cassie, stretching out a shivering eager hand.

'*What is this?*'

Everyone froze. The door had swung open and Ranjit stood there, rigid.

His cold eyes travelled from face to face, lingering on Richard and then on Katerina. Several of the Few got to their feet, and even the sixth formers looked a little sheepish. At last, shocked, angry, and for an instant dumbstruck, he looked at Cassie. 'What is she doing here?'

Man, he knew how to rile her – even if it was what she'd just been asking herself. Springing up, Cassie swung round, ready to fire off a few choice curses, but seeing his face, she found herself speechless.

A pulse was beating hard in his throat. Something else fleetingly crossed his expression, something Cassie couldn't quite define. Fear? Was he frightened? Of *her*?

Surely not.

For her?

Richard interrupted the silence. 'She's a candidate, Ranjit.'

'Oh, is she? I thought I'd made my views clear?'

Katerina slipped her arm through his, turning him firmly away from Cassie as she stroked his lapel. 'Come along, Ranjit, darling. I like your new suit. Is it Armani?'

Ranjit's lip curled. 'Mikhail, you look terrible. Go to your room.'

'Just what I've been telling him,' murmured Katerina, swiftly dropping the flattery.

The blond boy slunk from the common room, knuckles white around yet another water bottle. Ranjit didn't watch him go.

'Cassandra, please excuse us. Your proposer . . .' he gave Richard a savage glance, 'will take you back to your room.'

'Thanks,' she said sharply. 'I don't need an escort.'

'Richard.' Ranjit's tone had a distinct edge.

'Come on, Cassie.' Richard slung an arm round her shoulders, earning another filthy look from Ranjit. 'Let's go and find your – friend. Isabella, I mean.'

'Our decision will be made within a month,' smirked Katerina. 'Other candidates have to be interviewed, and final approval has to be sought from the Elders. We'll let you know.' She flapped her fingers in a dismissive gesture.

'You did well,' said Richard, as the door swung silently shut behind them and he led her along the bust-lined corridor.

'Good,' said Cassie dully. *That's not how I feel*.

'I think you've got a great attitude. And you know what? I don't think Isabella will mind that much, anyway. It's theoretical, isn't it? Just a case of showing your determination. Your ambition.'

'Ruthlessness,' muttered Cassie.

'If you like. But it won't come to that.'

I hope not, thought Cassie miserably. When she imagined how Isabella might react, she half-hoped the Few would reject her. But she also hoped violently that she'd be accepted.

Anyway, she told herself for the umpteenth time, she needed to know what they were up to. Finding things out, finding people out, taking care of herself: that was what had helped her survive Cranlake Crescent. That was what had got her out of there, and brought her here to Paris.

If she played her cards right, it would help her survive the Academy, too.

CHAPTER FOURTEEN

There had to be someone she could talk to. Cassie missed Patrick Malone and his cheerful good sense more than she had for weeks. He'd have known what to do. He'd have known what was *right*. But he wasn't here. She was on her own.

Unhappily, Cassie stole a sidelong peek at Isabella. She raised her head from her book and winked. Madame Lefèvre was enthusing about Proust, and there was a miasma of boredom in the overheated classroom. Outside the windows, an early-morning frost edged the bare trees.

Herr Stolz? No, she didn't know him well enough. Madame Lefèvre? Hardly. The other teachers? Some of them were downright intimidating; the science master Chelnikov was terrifying. The one person she'd have run to with any other problem was Isabella. And confiding in her, of course, was out of the question.

Sir Alric Darke? No way.

How about someone who was old enough to have seen and done it all, who knew all there was to know about the Academy? How about Madame Azzedine? The old woman seemed to like her. Somehow Cassie liked her too, and trusted her. She could talk to Madame Azzedine.

After all, there was a lot she wanted to ask. Alice's desk was still empty. Cassie hardly knew the girl, but in the last couple of weeks she'd found herself longing to see Alice return to classes. The longer she was absent, the more uneasy Cassie felt. At least Richard had stopped pretending it was a hangover.

'Poor old thing.' Yesterday in the café he'd only shrugged, and ordered Cassie another croissant. 'She's reacted very badly to that virus.'

'But has anyone called a doctor?'

'Of course. But she was as mystified as everyone else. A post-viral syndrome, she thought. Alice will get over it. She needs rest, that's all.' He'd jiggled his eyebrows. 'Come on, old girl, don't let it spoil your appetite.'

At least, thought Cassie, Mikhail Shevchenko was looking better. A lot better, actually. By the morning after Cassie's interview Mikhail had been in bouncing health again, cheeks glowing with colour, eyes bright and mischievous. There wasn't even a remnant of his weird raging thirst.

His poor old roommate Sasha was the one who'd looked drained. Up all night looking after Mikhail, probably.

That was one mystery she could have discussed with Isabella, except that Isabella could talk about nothing but her own interview. The embossed card had appeared under their door the day after Cassie's return from the common room. Same message, same time, different date.

'See? Isn't this wonderful?' Her roommate's face had fallen just a little. 'Only one vacancy, I know.' Her mercurial mood changed again, and Isabella had laughed with delight. 'But next time there is a vacancy, we shall both be members of the Few!'

Hell's teeth, thought Cassie, I hope not.

'Time, ladies and gentlemen!' Madame Lefèvre's severe voice interrupted her reverie. 'You have all seemed very distracted today. Please try to arrive tomorrow in a more *enquiring* frame of mind.'

Oh God, thought Cassie, if only you knew . . .

As they filtered out of the classroom, Cassie had to put a hand on Isabella's arm to slow her down. 'Hey, wait for me!'

'Oh, Cassie, I'm sorry. I'm excited, that's all!' The girl was like an uncorked bottle of champagne, about to fizz over.

'It's tonight.' A feeling of horror lodged in Cassie's stomach. Of course the interview was tonight. She'd known that. It had crept up on her, that was all, and she'd been trying not to think about it.

'Isabella.' She drew her friend to a halt. 'Do you really think you'd get on with that lot?'

Puzzlement flitted across Isabella's beautiful features. 'Cassie, do you mind that I am having an interview also?'

'No. No, of course not. I'm happy for you. It's just . . .' Cassie realised there was nothing she could say. All she was going to do was botch her friendship with Isabella, if she carried on in this clumsy direction.

'It's just I can't imagine either of us being Few.' Recovering, she gave Isabella a wink. 'They can be a bit . . .'

'Up themselves,' whispered Isabella, and they erupted into stifled giggles. 'Don't worry, Cassie. When we are both members – and we *will* be! – we shall change the culture! We shall be revolutionaries! We will make it fun to be Few!'

Dancing backwards a few steps, she laughed out loud and jogged for the stairs. Cassie followed, much heavier of heart.

169

Fun to be Few.

Right.

*

'You look fabulous.' Awed, Cassie stared at Isabella.

'You like it?' Isabella turned an elegant circle, letting the flaring silk of the Valentino dress swirl around her knees.

'It's beautiful. Honest.' Laying down her pen, Cassie raised an eyebrow. 'I'm not even going to ask how much it cost. I'd only faint and hurt myself.'

'True.' Isabella laughed. 'But I had to look good for my interview, didn't I? I spoke to Papa today and he is *very* excited, and he says I must make a splendid impression. He insisted I go out this afternoon and—'

As usual, Isabella's face darkened with remorse. She bit her lip hard. 'Oh, Cassie, I am so sorry. Always with you I say such stupid things. I have – what do you say – the tact of a . . .'

'Bulldozer? Brick?' Cassie grinned. 'Don't worry, for goodness' sake. I'm not a sensitive southern flower like you. Stop biting yourself, you'll ruin the lippy.'

'The . . . ?'

'The lipstick. Stop biting it.'

Isabella laughed, happy again. Honestly, thought Cassie, if you harnessed the girl's mood changes you could power Greater Manchester.

170

'I am sure I will not be chosen this time,' Isabella assured her, though her wide smile belied that. 'I am sure they will like you best. Just as I do! But soon, Cassie – soon, I swear, it will be two of us!'

'Course it will.' Cassie stood up and gave her the tightest hug she could manage without creasing the stunning dress. 'Isabella?'

'What?' Isabella hesitated at the open door, itching to go.

'I hope you get it,' Cassie lied. 'That's all. Good luck.'

*

It wasn't a spur of the moment thing. She'd been planning this ever since Isabella had received her invitation. She'd thought of everything, weighed up all the risks, and she'd known all along she couldn't pass up such a golden opportunity.

Keiko would be occupied with the interview. The Japanese girl didn't like Isabella; she'd want to be there – to scorn her, ask hard questions, make her look small. Cassie's own interview had lasted ages, even after half the Few had left. Of course, it would have taken a whole lot longer if the jumped-up Ranjit hadn't interrupted. He'd have no objections to a rich girl like Isabella, though, so tonight that wouldn't be a problem. All the Few would be together, closeted with Isabella in their oppressive common room.

There was never going to be a better chance to snoop. There was still the question of the Few's roommates, of course: roommates who might be awake, alert and in their rooms. All but one. One of the few had a chronically unwell roommate who might easily be quarantined in the sickroom . . .

She'd been over all this in her head a hundred times. It would be fine.

Stupid to have doubts now, then. Cassie shook her head and secured her unruly hair with a scrunchie, then bent to tie the laces of her trainers. Her heart was beating so hard she could barely breathe. What was she so afraid of? OK, what she was going to do was wrong. It was dishonest, and dishonourable too. It could get her expelled. But it was hardly going to get her killed.

Get a grip, Cassie!

Which reminded her . . .

Isabella spent as much on her hair accessories as she did on everything else, thought Cassie approvingly. The hair grips in her little walnut chest were expensive, strong but flexible, decorated with small gold lilies. As she slipped out of their room and through the quiet corridors, Cassie only hoped she wasn't going to ruin the one she'd chosen – but she'd got through locks with flimsy wire grips, screwdrivers and credit cards, and never snapped any.

She kept her expression vague and a little thick, and no one she passed took the slightest notice of her. At least she knew for certain that the Few would be occupied with Isabella's interview, and she could bluff her way past ordinary students and teachers any old day. The one person she was really afraid of running into was Marat the porter, but there was no sign of him.

Cassie wandered nonchalantly into the east corridor on the second floor. Alice and Keiko's room was easy to find: she knew roughly where it was, and how cooperative of the school to put nameplates on the doors.

Glancing quickly up and down the corridor, she leaned close to the door. Not a sound. No scratch of a pen, no rustle of a magazine, no murmur of a radio; not so much as a snore. Either the room was empty, or Alice was fast asleep and dead to the world. If she was sleeping, Cassie would slip away; she was good at moving silently in and out of rooms while other people slept. At least then she'd know Alice was OK. At least that would be reassuring.

If Alice *wasn't* there . . .Well, it would be a shame not to have a scout round.

Idly she tried the door handle. Locked, but she hadn't expected anything else. Twisting open Isabella's hair grip, she jiggled it into the lock. She could do this with her eyes shut. Literally. She could even do it while she leaned against the door, casually eyeing both ends of the corridor . . .

Inside the lock, the end of the grip caught something. One last wiggle, one last strong push and twist of her fingertips, and it gave with a muted *clunk*. Cassie held her breath for a long painful moment, but there was still no sound from the room beyond. She tried the handle again. Silently it gave, and the door swung open.

The light in the room was dim, cast by just one rose-pink shaded lamp, but Cassie could see Alice, lying on top of her bedcovers. She wore embroidered white cotton pyjamas, loose, beautifully clean and with an expensive sheen. She certainly hadn't been wearing those the whole time she'd been off sick. The girl lay on her side, facing the door, wild hair loose around her neck and across her forehead. Her hand was splayed in front of her chest, one leg hooked forward, almost as if she was in the recovery position.

Cassie could see all of that, in an instant, quite clearly. And she could see, too, that Alice's eyes were open. Panicked, she blurted an excuse, but Alice didn't so much as twitch. Her stare was so blank that for a hideous instant Cassie thought she was dead; then she heard her breathing, shallow and almost inaudible.

'Keiko?' mumbled Alice. 'That you?'

Swiftly, silently, Cassie closed the door.

'Keiko, please don't.' The voice was slurred, but Cassie could hear the tears that Alice was too weak to shed. 'Please, not again. 'S enough. Please?'

Cassie knew she shouldn't talk to her, but the girl looked so pathetic, she couldn't help herself. 'Alice. Alice, it's OK.' She crouched beside the bed and took Alice's limp hand.

'Keiko?'

'No. It's me, Cassie Bell. Alice?'

The girl didn't seem to have heard. 'Please don't . . .'

'Alice,' Cassie whispered urgently. 'Alice, I've got to help you. I don't know how. What do I do? Who do I call? Alice, please. Wake up. *Listen.*'

Wildly she glanced around the room. A mobile phone lay on the bedside table; Cassie flipped it open and scrolled down the directory. *Abbie. Granny Colette. Jack. Keiko. Mum . . .*

Mum? What would she say to Alice's mum? Would Mum have a clue what Cassie was on about? Would she even consider taking her seriously? *Nobody believed Cassandra. Nobody ever believed her.* Helplessly, Cassie realised she didn't know how mothers reacted in situations like this. Care home supervisors didn't count. Not the ones she'd had, anyway.

She suddenly felt like crying. Was that *self*-pity? she wondered contemptuously. Or was it that Alice looked so pitiful, lying there? The way she could hardly speak but she was begging anyway . . . Cassie stared at the highlighted *Mum*, finger hovering over the keypad.

The door handle vibrated. A key rattled in a lock that was already open.

Cassie spun round. A voice spoke outside, exchanging impatient pleasantries with someone in the corridor. She couldn't hear the words, but she'd know the voice anywhere.

Keiko.

CHAPTER FIFTEEN

'Now here's the thing.'

Keiko sat down on the edge of the bed. Taking Alice's limp fingers she absently massaged them, as if rubbing warmth back in. The Japanese girl herself looked . . . terrible. Almost as bad as Alice: pale, thin, exhausted. She seemed stooped, like an old woman. There was a faint odour from her that Cassie couldn't place.

'I'm developing. I'm hungry. It's – what can I say, a growth spurt.' Keiko gave a dry chuckle. 'I need you, but it won't last much longer, I promise. I've asked an Elder. It'll be over soon, and you'll be fine. You won't even remember this. That's why we ask you to drink.'

Cassie watched, horribly fascinated, from the darkness of the bathroom. The door was slightly ajar; she hadn't dared shut it as Keiko came in, in case the girl heard the click of the latch. Now she was afraid her heart must be audible, because it thudded painfully in her chest, blood pounding in her ears. Standing in the bath, pressed against the wall tiles and protected only by the clear glass shower door, she was hardly well hidden. Don't panic, she told herself. Stay still, and she'll leave.

Please don't let her need a pee . . .

Alice had stopped protesting. She still lay on her side, trying to curl in on herself, but Keiko took her shoulder and rolled her effortlessly on to her back. Alice stared past Keiko at the ceiling, shaking with terror.

'Now, shh. It'll be OK. I know you feel weak just now but Sir Alric told me you're very strong. You'll be fine.'

With that, Keiko crouched over Alice and kissed her.

Cassie's eyebrows shot up. Who'd have thought it? Oh well, what did the Parisians say? *Chacun à son goût* – each to his own . . . Though she'd kind of had the notion that Keiko fancied Perry Hutton.

Alice didn't respond to the kiss at all. Her body was trembling violently now. Forgetting her embarrassment, Cassie frowned. Keiko's kiss wasn't a tender one. Her lips fastened on Alice's, she was sucking on the girl like a demented Hoover.

Alice's bare feet jerked. The veins on them were stark and purple, standing out like thin dark wires, as if trying to burst through her skin. Her hand, thrashing beside Keiko in a futile protest, was the same. As Keiko drew back for breath, Cassie saw Alice's face clearly. That too was webbed with throbbing veins, pulsing towards her lips beneath skin that was paper-white. Tears had dried on her temples, as if she had no more left to cry.

Keiko snapped her head to the side, as if hearing something. She looked a lot better now. Soft, lovely skin. Glossy hair. Moist lips.

'It's fine,' she soothed, brushing her roommate's brow with her fingertips. 'I'm skilled, Alice, I don't make foolish mistakes. I've practised diligently. You won't be harmed. Not permanently.'

Alice was completely unresisting as Keiko bent to her mouth once more.

Cassie was glad of the cold hard tiles at her back. If they hadn't been there she thought she might have fallen, her legs felt so weak. She propped herself tighter into the corner, keeping her eyes on the two girls in the next room.

Keiko sucked on Alice's lips again, but this time only for a few seconds. Then her body went still and tense, her head lifted, and she tossed her shining black hair out of her eyes.

She was staring at the bedside table. She was staring at

the place where Alice's phone had been, where Isabella's golden hair grip now lay.

Oh, hell.

The bathroom door banged wide open, shuddering, and Keiko sprang towards Cassie like a hunting leopard. Something glinted in the girl's fist. Long, curved, pale. A blade.

Cassie slammed the glass shower door hard into Keiko as she leaped. Knocked off balance, Keiko yelled with rage, stumbling and sliding on the floor tiles. Cassie slammed the shower screen again, hard against the Japanese girl's head, then swung out as the glass did, leaping from the bath and scrambling for the bathroom door. A hand seized her ankle, incredibly strong, and panic choked her. Keiko had dropped her knife, but now she was clawing for it on the smooth tiles.

Flailing wildly, Cassie hammered Keiko's knuckles with Alice's phone, till the girl released her ankle with an animal scream. Cassie threw the phone at Keiko's face and ran. Banging the bedroom door behind her, she heard it flung open again almost immediately.

Run, Cassie, run. Just run.

The corridor was deserted. Bloody typical. Cassie bolted towards the stairs. Night had fallen. The wall sconces shone. How long had she been hiding, watching Alice?

Too long. Agile footsteps raced behind her, gaining, gaining.

Cassie snatched a rearing stone horse from a marble shelf and turned to fling it at Keiko, gasping with the weight of it. The girl halted, raising a hand, but she knocked the sculpture away like a pebble. The grin on her face was vicious, but what Cassie registered most clearly was her eyes. They were no longer beautiful, dark irises in clear whites. They were blood-red from corner to corner.

Keiko snarled, shifting her knife from one hand to the other, slashing out. Dodging, Cassie ran, stumbling down the stairs. The footsteps came after her, racing now. Through her gasps she heard a low laugh of glee, almost at her ear. Cassie vaulted over the banister, dropped awkwardly to the next flight, and ran again.

Don't let her catch you.

Cassie flung herself over the last banister rail and staggered to her feet in the entrance hall. Her lungs ached, terror froze her muscles. *She couldn't run fast enough.* Grabbing a marble arm for support, she swung herself under a statue and into the deep shadows. Cassandra and Clytaemnestra. How appropriate. *I smell blood now, all right.*

Something dropped gracefully to the tiles of the hall.

Cassie's breath shuddered in and out of her lungs. She had to stay still, so very still. But there was a high-pitched sound in her throat: her own terror. Keiko had stopped laughing. Thoughtful now, confident, she passed the knife to her left hand, and back to her right. Its blade gleamed evilly, but it was the hilt that caught Cassie's attention. The metal seemed to be in motion beneath Keiko's fingers, as if it was wriggling, squirming, straining for blood. Even through her chilling terror, Cassie was fascinated.

Standing quite still, Keiko raised her head and sniffed delicately at the air. She smiled.

Strolling casually to the statue, Keiko stroked the same marble arm Cassie had grabbed. As she reached into the darkness, Cassie heard her eager breath, smelled her expensive perfume. The sickly, dead scent of her was gone.

Closing her eyes, Cassie waited for the grip of a powerful fist, the bite of a blade. *Please don't let it hurt. Much.* She squeezed her eyes tighter against tears.

When Keiko screamed, she snapped them open again. It wasn't a scream of triumph, but of rage and confusion. Keiko stumbled back, half-falling, dragged by a boy clutching her hair in his fist. It took Cassie a bewildered moment to make out the figure behind Keiko.

Jake Johnson.

As Cassie scrambled from the shadows, he flung Keiko aside and grabbed Cassie's hand. 'Come on!'

'Wait!' Cassie spun round. Keiko had leaped swiftly to her feet. 'Jake!'

Gasping, he raised an arm to protect himself as Keiko sprang forwards. Ducking, Cassie rolled clear, then lashed out with a foot. *Missed.* She tried again, lunging for Keiko and grabbing her, but she was shaken off like a fly, falling hard to the floor. God, Keiko was strong.

As she staggered up, dazed, she saw Keiko and Jake locked together, Jake fighting to keep the blade away from the side of his neck. He was strong too, but Keiko was forcing the tip of the knife slowly towards his flesh, her lips peeled back in a horribly deliberate grin.

Once more Cassie leaped for Keiko's back, tearing at her hair. Yowling like a cat, Keiko clawed at her, and Jake took his chance, slamming her arm with all his strength into the statue, knocking the knife from her grip.

It clattered and spun on the floor. All three of them sprang for it simultaneously, but Jake shouldered clumsily into Keiko, knocking her off balance, while Cassie landed on her stomach on the floor, her nose an inch from the blade.

Her fingers fumbled on the knife hilt, slippery with sweat, but when they closed on it at last, it fitted perfectly in the palm of her hand. For a moment she gazed at it in wonder, almost hypnotised: then she came back to herself with Jake's yell. She rolled on to her back. Keiko was coming at her. Instinctively, thoughtlessly, she thrust the knife in front of her, just as Jake landed a flying kick between Keiko's shoulder blades. Keiko was flung forward on top of Cassie, her head crashing into Cassie's ribcage hard enough to knock the breath from her lungs.

Crazy with panic, Cassie forgot the knife, releasing it to shove and struggle frantically against the girl's surprising weight. Pushing her off, gasping, she scrambled to her feet and turned to face Keiko's next attack.

It didn't come.

Trying to stand, one foot sliding, Keiko slipped and fell again, then recovered, dragging herself on to all fours. The silence was horrible. Jake hauled Cassie to her feet, but neither of them could run.

Keiko threw back her head at an impossible angle, and with a lurch of horror Cassie saw the jutting handle of the knife. The blade wasn't visible. It was sunk to the hilt in Keiko's throat.

The beauty and life Keiko had sucked out of Alice was fading fast, her lips peeling back further and further in a snarling rictus. Her shirt frayed and disintegrated, giving Cassie a glimpse of the label before that too crumbled to nothing. As the skin beneath dried and shrivelled, Keiko's eyes glowed redder with mortal fury.

Then Cassie saw it: a mark on the girl's shoulder blade. Elaborate twisting lines, a pattern two inches in diameter. It was no brand, no tattoo. The lines were blinding, white hot.

Keiko scrabbled at the knife, desperate to pull it out of her rapidly decomposing flesh. Her hands were gnarled and clawlike, her nails yellow and sharp. Jake gripped Cassie's arm so tightly she thought her circulation would stop.

As Keiko slumped writhing to the floor, her hair shedding in dry hanks and shrivelling where it lay, she snatched weakly once more at the knife's hilt. The blade shifted, but no blood leaked out, only a whisper of light that dissolved in the air. The white-hot mark on her shoulder went out like a blown candle. With a long-drawn-out hiss, Keiko crumpled, and died. When Cassie made herself look back at the girl's eyes, they were gone.

It felt like an age before she could hear Jake breathing again. His body was trembling against her; she felt ice-cold herself. Keiko's shrivelled eyeless face was still fixed on theirs.

Jake swore. 'That can't be – can't be what killed . . .' His whole body shook violently.

Reality kicked in hard. 'We have to get out of here. Come *on*,' said Cassie. Cold and calm all of a sudden, she pulled him away from Keiko's remains.

'Wait.' Jake looked drained, but his trembling had stopped, and now he too was cool and determined. He hesitated briefly, then reached down to the thing on the tiles and withdrew the knife. The blade was dry and dusty.

Jake slipped it into his shirt. '*Now* let's go.'

CHAPTER SIXTEEN

'Hang on,' whispered Jake. 'Look.'

He pulled Cassie to a halt on the top landing overlooking the great hall. They both peered stealthily over the gilded banister.

Keiko was still discernible, a shattered smear of dust on the gleaming marble tiles. Now a figure stood thoughtfully over her corpse. It was hard to tell in the darkness, and the person was foreshortened by the angle, but Cassie was sure it was Marat. The porter had a mobile phone pressed to his ear, and something very pale draped over his arm. Talking inaudibly into his phone, he looked around the hall, then raised his ugly head to scan the shadows of the grand staircase. Cassie drew sharply back, pulling Jake with her.

Lights clicked on, doors opened, questioning voices were raised.

As they risked one more glance over the banister, there was a flash of white in the gloom below. Cassie and Jake exchanged a look. Marat had swiftly flung a linen sheet over what was left of Keiko.

Cassie shivered. 'Come on.'

*

'Where have you been?' Isabella leaped up as Cassie pulled Jake into their room and shut the door firmly. 'What is happening? I was so worried. What is going on, Cassie? *Jake?*'

Cassie rubbed her forehead. Fiercely she blinked back tears. Now was not the time to go soft. 'Isabella! Your interview. What happened?'

'It was fine. Fine,' said Isabella. 'We had drinks, they were friendly. We talked. For heaven's *sake*, Cassie, what—'

'How long were you there?' interrupted Cassie. 'How long was the interview?'

Isabella looked bemused. 'An hour, two hours? I didn't know the time had gone so fast. But then there was trouble, some kind of a disturbance just now, and I was sent away.' She paused. 'So I returned here, Cassie, to find you gone. Now will you tell me what is going on?'

'Keiko's dead,' blurted Jake.

That silenced even Isabella, though only for a moment. 'Dead? What do you mean, dead?'

'What do you think it means?' snapped Jake. He was pale.

Cassie put a warning hand on his arm. 'An – accident. It's hard to explain . . .'

Isabella had her hand over her mouth, but she moved it down to her throat. She swallowed. 'Try me.'

'We didn't mean— I didn't . . . Listen, she was trying to kill Cassie!' Jake put his head in his hands for a moment. 'Cassie, what happened before I showed up?'

She opened her mouth, but hesitated. It seemed like an insane nightmare, and she might not believe this story herself as soon as she tried to tell it out loud. But Jake was ashen and stunned, Isabella angry and curious.

Cassie took a deep breath. 'I went to Keiko's room. Picked the lock.'

'You did *what*?' exploded Jake.

'I wanted to find stuff about the Few. I just wanted to see if there was anything written down, any papers. And I was worried about Alice.' Cassie curled her lip, defiant. 'I reckon you'd have done the same. Mister *Sleepwalker*.'

'Oh, I would, if I'd had the nerve. I've tried to get into the common room before, but never one of their own rooms. You know how dangerous that was?'

'Oh yeah. Now I do. Keiko was eating Alice.'

'*What?*' Isabella yelped. 'Cassie!'

'I'm not kidding. I swear it. Keiko came in, and I had to hide, and I watched. She was . . . it was like she was *feeding* off Alice, something like that.'

'Like a vampire?' Isabella made a revolted face. 'That's weird. Some of the kids, they see this stuff on the internet and they—'

'No,' said Cassie impatiently. 'I mean, feeding off her energy. Sucking it out of her. I saw them both and I swear they weren't playing, it wasn't a game. Keiko was practically sucking the life out of Alice. No blood, not like that. Just . . . her *life*. And then she saw me. And then—' Cassie swallowed hard, 'that was when she came after me. With that knife.'

Isabella stared. 'What knife?'

Jake reached into his shirt. 'This kni—'

A fist thundered on the door.

The three of them looked at each other, frozen.

'Jake,' whispered Isabella. 'Jake has to hide. Now.'

'Cassie Bell! I know you are in there. Open this door, do you hear me?'

Cassie mouthed a curse.

Katerina.

'Bathroom,' whispered Isabella, and grabbed Jake's arm.

There was no time for Cassie to argue, no time for her to say what a lousy hiding place a bathroom made. As

Jake slipped in and flushed the loo, Cassie closed the door loudly and nodded at Isabella. Taking a deep breath, Isabella swung open the bedroom door, now shuddering under the blows of that determined fist.

Framed in the doorway, elegant with rage, Katerina looked like smouldering ice. If anything she was even taller, thought Cassie, and she didn't take a shred of notice of Isabella. Her blue eyes held Cassie's.

'Where have you been?' she hissed.

'That's right, you don't know where I've been.' Cassie smiled inanely at her. 'Best not to touch me without a bargepole.'

'Don't try to be clever, Miss Scholarship. What were you doing tonight? Where were you?'

Isabella folded her arms and glared at Katerina. 'Cassie has been most unwell. An upset stomach.' She cocked her head at the sound of the flushed cistern filling.

Cassie pulled a face. 'God, yes. I don't know who made the crêpes at dinner but—'

'Don't insult my intelligence.' Katerina's chest was heaving.

Why ever not? Cassie managed not to say it out loud. 'Of course I wouldn't.' She grabbed her stomach, grimacing. 'Here it comes again.'

'Cassie, darling.' With an expression of sympathy,

Isabella put an arm round her shoulders. 'Shall I fetch the nurse?'

'No, I'll be fine, I—' She gasped. *'Ohhhhh!'*

Katerina's teeth were gritted, but she looked from one to the other, hesitant. Human frailty obviously repelled her. 'If I find,' she hissed, 'if I *ever* find you saw something tonight you should not have seen, Cassie? Then it will be very bad for you. Do you understand?'

'Uh-huh? Why would there be anything I shouldn't see?' Cassie remembered to wince at another imaginary stomach cramp.

'I think you know, little prowler.' Katerina's lip twisted. 'You are like that pathetic, simpering fool Jake Johnson, always snooping where you shouldn't. Be careful what you look for, scholarship girl. One day you might find it.' She gave Cassie an unpleasant smirk. 'And then you will be sorry. So terribly sorry, and *too late*.'

'And I'm terribly sorry now, but you're going to have to excuse me.' Cassie put one hand on the bathroom door handle, the other over her mouth.

'Don't make the mistake of thinking me a fool,' breathed Katerina. She backed slowly away from Cassie. 'If you had anything to do with what happened to Keiko tonight, I promise you will pay. Do you understand me?'

'No.' Cassie pushed the bathroom door an inch

open, holding the icy gaze unflinchingly. 'What's happened to Keiko?'

Disgusted, Katerina stalked out and slammed the door.

Cassie rested her forehead against the bathroom door frame. They should be having a giggle now. They should be feeling triumphant at getting shot of Katerina. Remembering Keiko's fate, Cassie didn't feel like laughing any more, and obviously neither did Isabella. Miserable, Cassie watched her friend start to cry.

'Isabella.' Cassie clasped her cold fingers. 'I'm so sorry. I swear to God it was an accident. I'm so sorry it happened, but she was attacking me, and if Jake hadn't—'

'I don't feel sorry for Keiko.' Through her shocked tears, Isabella's tone was outraged. 'She tried to kill you! Oh, Cassie, what if she had?'

'She didn't.' Jake had emerged from the darkness of the bathroom. He propped himself against the door, still trembling, staring at the place where Katerina had stood.

'Thanks to you,' pointed out Cassie.

'Sure. Maybe not a completely simpering fool, huh?' He folded his arms.

'Oh, Jake.' Isabella hugged herself, digging her fingers into her arms as if to avoid hugging him instead. 'I'm sorry. Truly I am. I'm so sorry you heard that.'

And she really was, thought Cassie, amused and touched. The sensitive southern flower was worried about *his* feelings. Isabella was well smitten.

''S OK.' Jake shrugged. 'I guess I've been kind of starry-eyed, haven't I?'

'That is because you are kind,' insisted Isabella fiercely. 'You are not like her! *You* would not dream a person could be cruel and unpleasant and . . . scheming. It is not how your mind works!'

'Nice of you to say so, Isabella.' He gave her a weak smile and shrugged. 'But I think maybe I'm just dumb. Y'know? My brains being down in my—'

'No!' exclaimed Isabella, mortified. 'Do not say such a thing about yourself!'

Whoa! That was rich!

'Um,' said Cassie dryly. 'If you two could break it up for a minute?'

'OK.' Jake grinned.

Cassie took a breath. 'What are you up to, Jake Johnson?'

Swearing, he rubbed his temples with finger and thumb.

'I mean,' Cassie went on, 'everybody round here seems to be up to something. But you're not – well, even if you do have a bad sleepwalking problem, I don't think you're

194

up to anything really bad. Right?' She sank her teeth in her lip.

Jake sat down on the floor and clasped his hands behind his neck. After a pause he said, 'Something's wrong at this school.'

Cassie snorted. 'That much I'd gathered.'

'Jake.' Isabella slumped down on her bed and leaned towards him full of concern. 'It's Jessica, right?'

Unhappily he nodded.

'What? *Jake*.'

'I need to find out who killed her. *What* killed her.' He went quiet for a minute. 'OK? I need to know.'

The silence was so thick that Cassie wanted to fling open the window and let in the night air.

'Jake,' said Isabella gently. 'I know how upset you were – are – but it wasn't . . .' She took a deep breath and whispered, 'It could have been an accident.'

'It wasn't an accident. Somebody killed her.' He gave Cassie a sober look. 'Some*thing* killed her.'

'But you cannot take it upon yourself to—'

'So who else is going to? Darke? The police? The Cambodian police weren't interested. Nobody is. She was only a scholarship, wasn't she?'

Cassie shuddered.

'Jess wasn't the first, either,' said Jake.

'It's the school's bad luck,' put in Isabella. 'A jinx. That's what they say.'

'Some jinx.'

'And Sir Alric – listen, you can't blame him. He was terribly upset when it happened. And he gave you the scholarship, Jake, in her memory.'

'To keep my family quiet, you mean. To repair the PR damage. Mom might have fallen for his charity stunt, but I sure didn't. I took the scholarship so I could find out what happened to Jess.'

'So what have you found out?' said Cassie.

'Not a lot.' Jake's voice was bitter. 'It's to do with the Few, that's all I know. One of them killed her, and I reckon I know which one. I need to prove it, that's all.'

'If you prove a murder,' said Isabella, 'if it gets out that a student was killed here, that it was covered up, it'll be the end of the Academy.'

'Uh-huh.' Jake shrugged. 'I want to close this place down, Isabella, that's the truth. That's why I don't expect you to like what I'm doing. Just, please, don't tell anyone.'

Isabella sprang to her feet. 'You think I'm such a spoilt heiress, hey? Tell, indeed! I should slap you, Jake Johnson.'

'Well, I—'

'You think I'd throw a hammer in the works?'

'Spanner,' said Cassie absently.

'Yes, yes. You think I'd ruin it for you because I like my school? I liked Jessica a lot more. If somebody killed her I want him – her – *them* – caught. If you think something is sinister here, Jake, if you think somebody at the Academy was responsible for what happened to Jess, then I'm not staying out of it.'

Bemused, he said, 'Hang on a minute—'

'Shut up,' she told him crisply. 'Stupid American. Don't be so proud. Don't be such an isolationist. We are going to help you. Yes, Cassie?'

'Oh, yeah.' Cassie grinned at Jake. 'She's right, know that?'

'I am always right.' Isabella sniffed.

Cassie dug her in the ribs. 'Three of us can get where one can't. That's obvious, uh-huh? We can do three times more. And after what I saw tonight?' She shivered. 'I think you need all the help you can get, Jake.'

'And *I* am a little princess with a rich papa and good contacts.'

Jake chewed manically on a knuckle. 'Could be dangerous.'

'Danger,' Isabella tossed her hair, 'is my middle name.'

'OK. OK!' Jake gave a bark of laughter. 'Know what? I'm glad I ran into you tonight, Cassie.'

'Not half as glad as I am,' she said dryly. 'Jake, who do you think killed Jess?'

'I don't *know*. I can't prove it, not for certain. But Ranjit knew where she was that night.'

Cassie's stomach contracted. 'He did? Are you sure?'

'Yes. And Ranjit and Jess were . . . Well, they had a thing together. Maybe they had a fight, maybe there was someone else and he got jealous, I dunno. It's the likeliest explanation, isn't it? I've tried to ask him to explain, but he won't talk about it. Won't even discuss the Few. He's hiding something. Maybe he's just sick.'

Cassie felt sick herself. 'But what d'you mean, "He knew where she was"?'

Jake's face set cold. 'Because he was the one who found her. Ranjit found Jess's body.'

CHAPTER SEVENTEEN

'I feel so guilty. If I hadn't been ill, who knows? I might have noticed something was wrong. I might have been able to help her.'

The tearful English accent was familiar. Cassie came to a halt and turned quickly on her heel in front of the noticeboard. The voices were just round the corner, approaching through the entrance hall.

'You mustn't blame yourself, Alice.' The other girl had a lilting accent. Ayeesha?

'I can't help it. Such a terrible thing to do. She must have been desperate, I should have noticed something. Somebody at breakfast said that she looked awful, not herself at all. Oh, I should have *noticed*—'

'Now, now.' Yes, it was definitely Ayeesha. 'People can be very skilled at hiding these things, and Keiko must have been very determined. To jump from the upper floor! Please, Alice. There was nothing you could have done.'

Cassie peered closely at a Christmas Ball notice as the two girls came round the corner, but Ayeesha stopped and put a hand on her arm.

'Cassie, hello!' Ayeesha smiled.

'Oh. Hi, Ayeesha! I was miles away.' Oh dear, thought Cassie: not very convincing. 'Hello, Alice.' She swallowed awkwardly. 'Are you OK?'

'Yes, I suppose.' Alice was almost in tears. Her face was stunned and a little panicked. 'No. Terrible. I just want to go to classes.'

'But this morning – you sure that's a good idea?'

'I need to be busy. I've missed so much, it'll keep me occupied.'

Ayeesha shook her head. 'I think classes are going to be cancelled, Alice. But we'd better be on time anyway. Come on, Cassie.'

Cassie walked alongside Alice. 'I'm so sorry about Keiko.'

'Me too.' Tears spilled down Alice's cheeks.

Hell, thought Cassie, bewildered. It was obvious Alice had no memory of what Keiko had been trying to do to her, just last night. 'You're feeling better, though? Are you sure? I mean, you've got over your . . . ?'

'Glandular fever.' Alice blew her nose. 'Couldn't have happened at a worse time, could it? And all I hear is how worried Mummy is about *me*. How Daddy's employed a tutor to help me catch up in the holidays. They've been on the phone since half past five this morning but they don't seem to care about Keiko. It's all about me. Am *I* OK. When poor Keiko . . .' Alice put her hand over her mouth.

Cassie scrutinised Ayeesha, but she was all sympathy for Alice. 'Well. It can't have sunk in yet. And they'll be so worried about you.'

'God, yes. Mummy's had to book herself into a spa for a week. To help her nerves, you know?'

Ayeesha glanced dryly at Cassie as she shepherded Alice into Herr Stolz's classroom. 'You need a week in one yourself. Come and sit down, Alice.'

She wasn't kidding, thought Cassie as she sat down by Isabella. Alice still looked terrible – gaunt, pale and tired – though not nearly as fragile as the day before; Keiko's death must have begun to restore her straight away. Cassie could understand why she needed to get back to normality, why she needed to get out of her room. She probably understood Alice's motives better than Alice did. Glandular fever and the supposed suicide of a roommate weren't all she needed to escape.

Herr Stolz coughed, silencing the subdued murmur of the students, and got straight to the point. 'You are all aware by now of the terrible tragedy that occurred last night.' He was pale too, quite drained and shocked. 'You won't be surprised to learn that classes are cancelled for today and tomorrow.'

They all listened in silence, even the Few. Cassie had already noticed Ranjit was missing. *Again?* This time, Katerina was too. She stared out of the window, Herr Stolz's voice fading to a murmur. She couldn't concentrate; there were too many questions, too many half-remembered conversations starting to fit together.

Why, for example, was Ranjit such a special case? He seemed to treat the school as his personal fiefdom, even more than the rest of the Few, to act as if classes were for lesser mortals. Somehow it didn't fit that Jessica had been his girlfriend. If Jess was anything like Jake, Cassie couldn't imagine her and Ranjit together. It would be as weird as picturing herself and Ranjit . . .

Her spine chilled. She looked like Jess: everyone said so.

The way you make me feel . . . I can't accept it, Cassandra.

What did that mean? He couldn't accept it, because he'd been in love with Jess? Or because he'd killed her?

Ranjit had warned Cassie off. Ranjit didn't want her in

202

the Few, when even the bitchy Katerina was willing to accept her. What made him dislike her so much? *Guilty conscience?*

Jess had gone in the night to Angkor Wat, and she'd never been seen alive again. What must it have been like for her, alone and scared in the jungle darkness? Hearing the soft approach, a killer drawing closer in the night . . .

He found Jess's body.

'. . . and we will all miss her.'

Cassie jumped. It took her a moment to realise Herr Stolz was talking about Keiko.

'The Christmas Ball will not be cancelled, but a minute's silence will be observed at the beginning. Sir Alric has asked me to let you know that arrangements will be made for a memorial service at a date early next term. In the meantime, any students who feel the need to talk to a senior member of staff should feel free to do so. Alice.' He smiled kindly at the English girl. 'This is a particular shock for you. I know you are keen to catch up on your studies, and work can be a good distraction. Please stay behind for a few minutes. The rest of you are free to spend today and tomorrow as you wish. Naturally there will be no boisterous behaviour.' He surveyed them all severely. 'Perhaps a study visit to a chapel or a cathedral would be more appropriate than the avenue Montaigne?'

Jake leaned across to Cassie and Isabella as they gathered their books and the murmur of gossip and speculation rose around them. 'Nôtre Dame, then, you guys? Eleven o'clock?'

Cassie made a doubtful face. 'Half the school might be there after that speech.'

Jake grimaced. 'Half the school will be in the avenue Montaigne flexing their gold cards, whatever Stolz says.'

'How about the Bois de Boulogne?' put in Isabella. 'A serene place for thought and reflection, no? Plenty of space. Plenty of privacy.'

'Good thinking. I'll meet you both at the Lac Inférieur.' Jake gave Isabella a wink. 'By the boats.'

*

'I'm freezing,' moaned Isabella. 'I shall freeze to *death*.'

'Cheer up, my southern flower.' Jake hauled on the oars. 'This was your brilliant idea. Anyway, you can die spectacularly of pneumonia, and someone will write a great tragic opera about you.'

Isabella gave him a teeth-chattering grimace, but her expression turned dreamy and distant as if she was already imagining her last heart-rending aria. Cassie cleared her throat in exasperation. 'Can we *not* talk about spectacular deaths?'

Jake's smile faded as he rested the oars in the rowlocks. 'I think we have to, huh?'

'How can anyone believe Keiko killed herself?' complained Isabella, wrapping her vicuña scarf once more round her neck and tucking her fingers under her arms. 'I thought you said she had a knife in her throat?'

'Not by that time.' As the little boat drifted under the frosted chestnut trees, Jake fumbled inside his jacket and drew out Keiko's knife. Its blade was wrapped up in strips torn off an old T-shirt, and it took him a minute to unwind them. Tentatively he held the knife out in two hands. The girls stared at it, riveted.

'Marat covered her body before anyone came,' Cassie told Isabella. 'We saw him do it. After everyone was sent back to bed, he must have moved it, fast.'

'*They* must have moved it,' corrected Jake. 'Marat can't be the only one involved. Somebody else must have seen that body.'

'And who exactly are *they*?' murmured Cassie.

The lake was still, and the boat shifted only a little on the water as they fidgeted in the cold. Feathers of ice were forming on the surface, and Isabella trembled. Cassie wasn't that cold, but she shivered too as she examined the knife blade. It was some six inches long, slightly curved, the edge smooth and gleaming in the wintry December light.

December. It was the first of December. Cassie could hardly believe it. She'd been at the Darke Academy nearly a whole term. Boy, she'd learned a lot . . .

'Look at the handle,' said Jake. 'It's weird. I've never seen anything like it.'

'Nor me, said Isabella. 'And Papa collects antique swords, daggers, things like that. I'm sure he could tell us something about it, but I have seen nothing like this one in his collection.'

Cassie reached out to touch the handle. It felt ancient. The elaborate carvings seemed smoothed by centuries, sheened with age. She stroked the pad of her forefinger along them. You had to inspect the handle closely to see the details, because all the figures and beasts and ornamentation were intertwined: snakes, mermaids, caryatids, demons – snarling, twisted things that might have been cats or wolves.

'I bet it's worth a fortune,' she remarked. 'Y'know, at night it looks incredible. There's sort of an optical illusion. The carvings seem to move.'

'They're so realistic, aren't they?' Isabella touched the knife, then snatched her hand back. 'I don't like it, though.'

'I do,' said Cassie.

'I don't like it or dislike it.' Jake rewrapped the blade and tucked it back inside his jacket. 'It's evidence, that's all.'

'Evidence of what?' said Cassie. 'That's not proof of anything, unless Keiko's wacky DNA's on it. Or ours. And then it's you and me in trouble, cowboy.'

'I know, I know. But there must be more to find.'

Sniffing, Isabella rubbed her nose violently. It was turning red. 'Well. How do we find more? Where to start?'

'We need connections with the Few, that's obvious.' Jake frowned. 'They're at the heart of it.'

Isabella shrugged. 'Cassie and I have both been interviewed. At least one of us must be chosen.'

He shook his head. 'I don't like that idea.'

'Yeah, but you're not calling the shots, are you?' said Cassie. 'What's the worst that can happen? One of us gets to be a member, we find out as much as we can, then we say it was a mistake, we don't have the time, we need to study . . . something. Resign from the Few.'

'I don't think anybody gets to resign from the Few,' said Jake.

'I have never heard of it,' agreed Isabella. She took a deep breath. 'What about Ranjit?'

Jake froze. 'What about him?'

'He is the most important. He is practically Head Boy. They are all afraid of him, haven't you noticed? And I think he likes Cassie. He has the – what do you say? – the hots for her.'

'You're wrong,' muttered Cassie. 'He can never wait to get out of my company.'

'I don't think that is true, you know. I have seen how he stares at you.'

'That's because of how she looks,' said Jake bitterly. 'She's the ghost at his cosy little banquet. No way can Cassie get involved with him. It's too dangerous. Who knows what he'd do if she got too close? Maybe that's what happened to—' He fell silent.

Isabella rubbed her arms. 'Richard, then?'

Sighing, Cassie trailed a finger through the icy skin on the water, till she realised the others were still watching her in silence. 'Look, Richard doesn't have much influence,' she protested. 'Some of the Few don't think he should have proposed me. Ranjit doesn't like him, and Katerina treats him like a pet. He probably doesn't know anything worth knowing.'

'He's still our only point of contact,' said Jake. 'And he *definitely* likes you. If he isn't in on the main clique, you could at least get friendly with the others through him.'

'Get him to take you to the Christmas Ball,' suggested Isabella. 'That would not be difficult.'

'Yeah?' snapped Cassie. 'If it's that easy, why doesn't *Jake* ask him to the flaming Christmas Ball. Richard fancies him too, doesn't he?'

'Look, I know you feel bad about using him,' said Jake, 'but Richard would use you if he needed to. That's what he's like. He wouldn't have a moment's hesitation, Cassie.'

'I'm not so sure. He's OK, you know. Richard.' Her cheeks were burning, even in the frosty air.

'It'd be safer than trying to get information out of Ranjit,' pointed out Jake.

Cassie sighed, beaten. 'I'll try, then, OK? But I'm not promising anything.'

'I appreciate it. Thanks, Cassie.' Lifting the oars, Jake began to pull the boat back round a little island and towards shore. 'You know we're the only idiots out in a boat?'

'I am not surprised,' Isabella sniffled. 'The boatman, he thought we were crazy people.'

'We are crazy people,' murmured Cassie. 'Do we know what we're getting into?'

'Hell, no!' Jake grinned. 'Life's a challenge, huh?'

A loud burst of music made them all jump, and the

boat rocked slightly. Cassie fumbled with cold hands in her coat pocket.

'Sorry,' she said sheepishly, pulling out her phone and staring at the display. She raised her eyebrows. 'You're not going to believe who this is.' She flipped it open. 'Hi, Richard.'

Jake hunched forward, letting the oars rest and drip water. Isabella huddled closer to Cassie, trying not to let her teeth chatter too loudly.

'The Bois de Boulogne, if you can believe it . . . Yeah, it's bloody cold.' Cassie laughed and bit her lip. 'With Isabella . . .' A small hesitation. '. . . and Jake . . . Yeah, well, I didn't see you after class was cancelled . . . Yes, course I looked. You'd gone.' Making a face at Jake, she crossed her fingers.

There was a moment's silence on the other end of the phone, and Cassie pressed it closer to her ear, a little anxious. 'Of course I'm not avoiding you. Where did you go anyway? Oh! Nôtre Dame!' Cassie raised an eyebrow at Jake, and he brushed imaginary sweat from his forehead in relief. 'I didn't think you were that obedient . . .'

After another pause, she laughed again. 'Course I will. What time? . . . That sounds great, Richard. Anyway, see you later, probably.'

She snapped the phone shut. 'Mission accomplished,' she said, a little unhappily.

'Mission in motion,' said Jake darkly. 'Hardly accomplished. You got a date?'

'The Arc de Triomphe. Tomorrow. It's a really special day, he says. He wants to show me something spectacular. I feel like a worm.'

Isabella patted her hand. 'Listen, sound him out carefully, hm? Maybe he will even want to help us.'

'Maybe.'

Jake pulled hard on the oars again. 'Thanks, Cassie. A lot. You're doing the right thing, you know that.'

'I know that.' Uneasily she surveyed the wintry parkland.

'So don't worry,' Jake chivvied. 'It's only a date. What can go wrong with that? And you don't have to do anything you don't want to do.'

'Yeah. I dunno, though.' Cassie licked her lips; they felt dry and cracked in the frosty air.

'Don't know what?'

'I've got a really bad feeling about tomorrow.'

CHAPTER EIGHTEEN

'Incredible, isn't it?' Richard squeezed her shoulders.

Setting behind the Arc de Triomphe, the sun was a golden fire. As the dazzle intensified, it lit the edges of the Arc and turned into a halo of flame. The whole structure seemed ablaze.

Catching her breath, Cassie felt Richard's fingers move towards her neck. She couldn't speak, but she wasn't sure if that was down to desire or fear.

'It's the anniversary of the Battle of Austerlitz. Napoleon's greatest victory. The one day every year when the sun sets in line with the Arc and the Champs-Elysées. *Magnifique,*' he murmured in her ear, '*n'est-ce pas?*'

'You bet,' she breathed.

They stood immobile until the light faded and the tourists around them had pocketed their digital cameras and dispersed in a babel of languages. Richard still held her tightly, and Cassie felt weak.

'Come on, or we'll miss the view!' He broke into a run up the Champs-Elysées. Cassie ran after him, but he didn't even slow down as he approached the maelstrom of traffic beneath the Arc.

'Are you crazy?' she yelled. She slid to a halt as he ran out between cars and motorcycles, oblivious to the blare of horns. For a fraction of a second she hesitated, but it seemed like a challenge, and she'd half-caught his madness. Grinning, she took a deep breath and pelted out through the traffic.

Insanity. She didn't know how she made it through. The screech of tyres and the scream of horns almost deafened her, the strobing headlights half-blinded her, but she felt like some fish or bird with a sixth sense, as if nothing could touch her. And she was right, she thought with a surge of fierce delight, as she hurdled the row of low bollards around the Arc. Dammit, she was immortal tonight!

'Cassie Bell, I knew you were perfect!' whooped Richard, seizing her and whirling her round. 'I knew it!'

'Sure I am,' she gasped. 'But we're going to get arrested.'

'Nah. Come on!'

The golden glow was gone from the stone, and from its

213

elaborate carvings and friezes. Instead, floodlights gave the Arc a ghostly aura, casting horses and soldiers into eerie relief. There was a chill in the air; it was getting late. Now the roar of traffic seemed far away.

'Two hundred and eighty-four steps,' he laughed. 'I'll race you!'

God, he was fit. Gamely, Cassie kept up with him as he took the first hundred steps up inside the Arc two at a time, and she wasn't so far behind when he stumbled out at the top and pulled her after him. Recovering her breath, she watched the blue night fall on Paris. She didn't know if the obstruction in her throat was down to the view or to her nagging guilt, but even the facetious Richard seemed struck sober. In the dusky air, it seemed as if every detail of the city came alive. Distantly, Sacré Coeur gleamed above Montmartre like a white pearl.

'Told you you'd like it,' he whispered.

She swallowed. 'It's amazing.' She liked him too, that was the trouble.

'You want to see something even better than this? Even better than the sunset?'

'Come off it.'

'No, really. I'm serious. There is something better. Trust me!'

She realised that for the last hour she'd forgotten what

she was supposed to be doing. In the dimming evening, as traffic swirled around the Arc and the city sparked into colour and life, it was hard to read Richard's expression. *Don't trust him*, Jake had said. But she couldn't help it. She shook her head.

'Course I trust you. It'll have to be pretty amazing to beat all this, though.'

'Believe me, it's more than pretty amazing.'

Reluctantly Cassie let him drag her away from the silver spiky railings and back to the steps. 'What's the hurry?'

'You have a great head for heights, don't you?'

'Uh-huh. Can you slow down a bit, though?' Head for heights or not, she wouldn't want to stumble and fall on the stairs, yet Richard was springing down them so fast she could hardly keep up. Brimming with excitement, he could hardly contain himself and he didn't seem to have heard her. Cassie yanked hard on his hand.

'Whoa!' she panted crossly, managing to drag him to a halt.

'Sorry!' He gave her a sweet, apologetic smile. 'Got carried away.'

'So did I, nearly. Take it easy, there's loads of time.'

'Not as much as you think.' His eyes were so bright they were almost feverish. 'Come on!'

She let go of his hand, feeling safer that way as she ran down the steps behind him. He dodged nimbly past other tourists, his enthusiasm infectious, and she found herself laughing as they jumped together to the bottom.

'I'm waiting for the revelation,' she teased.

'Almost there, Cassie Bell.' He grinned at her and blew a lock of dark hair out of his eyes. 'Are you ready for the surprise of your life?'

'Am I going to like it?'

'That depends on you. But I reckon I know you quite well.'

'So what do you reckon,' she said, 'knowing me so well?'

'Babe, I think you're going to love it!'

His fingertips hooked round a corner of stone, delicately stroked the edge of a huge block. As he glanced around a little nervously, so did she, but there were fewer tourists here beneath the arch, only a small party absorbed in the flickering flame on the Tomb of the Unknown Soldier and distracted by their guide.

Richard gave her a solemn wink, and pushed gently, and the block of stone swung silently wide.

She gaped. 'What the—'

'Shh! Quick!' He squeezed her arm. 'Go on, or they'll see us!'

'But where does it—'

'There's gendarmes over there,' he whispered. 'Hurry up!'

She swore, giggling, and pushed past him to edge into the darkness of the chamber. Swiftly he eased in after her, fumbling at the stone again from the inside until the hidden door swung shut again.

The blackness was solid, the cold gripping. Cassie shut her eyes and opened them again, but it made no difference. There was a faint smell of dry stone and fragrant smoke, a sweetness in the air that was not entirely pleasant. Cassie's heartbeat quickened.

'Richard?' Her voice echoed eerily.

'It's OK, I'm here. Hang on a sec.' With the rasp of a Zippo lighter, a flame leaped into life. Cassie blinked.

Stone walls, faintly golden like the Arc, closed in on her from two sides, but surprisingly she couldn't make out the ceiling: it receded too far into the shadows. At their backs the door was solidly shut, but the darkness beyond the flame wound downwards with no limit in sight. Obviously there was a passageway: a long one. Cassie held her breath, straining to listen. Was that a faint rustling, or . . . slithering?

Dumb thing to think. She rubbed her arms briskly. 'This is . . . amazing. But I'm not sure I love it.'

'Wait. There's lights, proper ones. If I can just find the . . . ah. Let me go past.' He squeezed past her in the narrow chamber, and turned, smiling at her expectantly in the dancing Zippo flame.

'The switch?' she prompted.

An explosion of pain in her head. Her whole body snapping forward. The stone floor slamming up to meet her.

And then even the last light, from the small brave flame, went out.

CHAPTER NINETEEN

A headache like nothing she'd ever felt. It sawed into her brain like a cold knife and when she tried to open her eyes, the light burned. She squeezed them shut again, feeling another lance of pain. Migraine? She didn't get migraines. Had she been drinking? She tried to roll on to her side and fumble for a paracetamol.

No. She couldn't move. Her arms were stretched above her head and she couldn't shift them. When she tried, sharp stabs raced through her shoulders, and something cut into her wrists.

She opened her eyes again. Her vision was blurred, but she could make out that the room was not terribly bright at all. The wall sconces were dim, flickering.

There's lights! Let me go past . . .

Richard. She remembered. Oh God.

She tried to kick out. That was no good either; her feet

were restrained too. She was stretched tightly on some kind of stone table, smooth and hard beneath her back. She still wore her jeans and her thin T-shirt, but she was barefoot, and bitterly cold. Her hooded top and her jumper were gone. Panicking, she writhed again, and metal bit against her wrists and ankles. She gave a sharp cry of fear.

A hand stroked her forehead. She tried desperately to focus, still fighting her bonds.

'Hush, now. Quiet. Don't hurt yourself. We don't want you hurt, Cassie.'

The male voice was muffled by some kind of hood. She thought she knew who was speaking, but she couldn't be sure. Nor could she answer, since her breathing was harsh and high-pitched and panic tightened her throat.

'Does your head hurt? I'm so sorry that was necessary.'

Cassie tried to focus, tried not to panic. That faint scent of fragrant smoke was stronger now, but whatever was burning, it didn't take the edge off the chill.

'We were afraid you'd resist. It looks as if we were right.'

She sensed a smile beneath the dark crimson hood, but there was no way of knowing for sure, since the only holes in it were narrow eye slits. 'Don't worry. Soon you won't feel such pain. Not ever again.'

That remark dried her mouth altogether. She licked her lips, but it didn't help. 'Am I going to die?' she managed to croak.

Laughter. 'What a ridiculous idea.'

'Is it?'

'Of course it is. Cassie Bell, you're not just going to *live*. You're going to live as you've never lived before.'

The figure stepped back, so that she could see up into the darkness of the chamber. Now that her eyes had adjusted, she could make out most of it. The torches cast leaping shadows on to the ceiling, where she could make out carved creatures in the stone. They reminded her of something else, if only she could think straight.

Oh, yes. The knife. The monsters and demons above her were like the ones carved on that ancient hilt. And just like those ones, the carvings above her seemed to move.

No, they didn't *seem* to move. They *were* moving. Biting back a scream, Cassie fought and tugged on her bonds, feeling blood on her wrists, blood on her ankles, and not caring.

'That's enough. Shh. You are not *permitted* to hurt yourself.' The voice was stern as someone else stepped forward, and Cassie went still. Struggling made her head hurt too much anyway. With an effort she turned her aching head to meet another slitted gaze, another crimson hood.

'I'm so pleased for you.' This time the distorted voice was feminine, the accent tantalisingly familiar. 'So pleased, Cassie. We shall be great friends.'

The hooded girl wore a key on a long gold chain around her neck. Behind her stood more sinister shapes. There was a whole circle of them. At least one of them wasn't disguised.

'*Richard?*'

The uneasy guilt left his face. With a forced grin he stepped forward, stretching out a hand to touch her manacled ones. When she only stared back, he linked his fingers through hers, and squeezed nervously.

'Good news, Cassie! You've been chosen!'

'I've been *what*?' This time she managed to bark it.

'Chosen. Accepted! You're one of us now. One of the Few!'

'Not quite yet,' murmured the first figure. 'But soon.'

'Cassie, I knew, didn't I? Didn't I tell you you'd be perfect? You're chosen!'

She spoke through clenched teeth. 'What if I don't want to be chosen?'

A harsh voice broke in, scornful. 'You offered yourself willingly. You attended a Congress to be interviewed.'

'I never heard there was a vote. I wasn't told.'

'There was no vote.' Richard sounded uncomfortable. 'The proposal was vetoed from on high, so this Congress is . . . ah, an unofficial one. But you've been favoured by a very influential member of the Few. That's more than enough.'

'Despite any petty school rules,' someone added.

Unofficial? What was that supposed to mean?

'And once you are Few, you will always be Few. There's nothing Sir Alric can do about that.'

Cassie caught her breath. 'You mean Sir Alric doesn't *know*?'

'You are very privileged.' Another cool voice spoke from the circle. Again she couldn't put a face to it. It was infuriating, but trying to work out their identities made her a little calmer. 'Membership of the Few has never been a func—'

'A function of scholarships,' spat Cassie, trembling. 'So what is their function, then?'

'Once you are Few, you'll know all there is to know. You won't regret it.'

'I get the feeling I will,' muttered Cassie.

The first hooded figure nodded at someone behind her. Suddenly Cassie remembered Alice lying helpless, too weak even to cry, feet and fingers jerking as her veins stood out on her skin . . .

'Richard,' she whispered. Tears sprang to her eyes, and Cassie hated herself for looking so weak in front of the Few. 'Don't let them do this. Please. Whatever it is. Please.'

His fingers tightened on hers. 'Cassie, darling! Hush! I know you're scared. I was too!'

She stared at him, dumbstruck, then licked her lips. 'This is what happened to you?'

'Of course. It's happened to all of us, Cassie. It's not so bad. Hah!' He laughed out loud. '*Not so bad?* Oh, it's so much better than that!'

'But I don't want this!' she screamed hoarsely.

'That's what I thought. I thought I didn't want it, but wait till you feel it inside you! There's nothing like it!'

'*What the hell is IT?*'

He hesitated. 'Don't worry. Accept it! Enjoy it, darling!'

Don't trust him, Jake had said. *He'd use you, you know that*. She gave another fierce jerk on her hands, though it took all her energy. Richard tutted and leaned closer to dab at the blood on her wrists. With as much effort as she could manage, she focused and spat.

Spot on. Right in the bastard's eye. She smiled.

Wiping his cheekbone, Richard stepped sadly away.

'She has no manners,' drawled another, all-too-familiar

voice. 'None at all. I can't think why—'

'Now, Katerina. It is agreed.'

Painfully Cassie rolled her head round. Katerina wasn't hooded either, and she was loving this, the cold-blooded cow. At the sound of footsteps, the chill of a draught from an opening door, Katerina turned.

The line of Few moved, parting as if letting someone enter, and when the circle closed again it had shrunk a little. Again they drew closer, then again. The ring was tightening like a noose. Cold terror gripped Cassie's gut. Which one was Ranjit? Which of them had killed Jess?

She couldn't see behind her, but she could feel the new presence. However she strained her neck, scraping her scalp on the stone, she couldn't tilt her head far enough to find out who was there. Her breathing grew faster, and she tried not to whimper. *Don't give them the satisfaction* . . .

'It's time.' Lifting the gold key from around her neck, the hooded girl unlocked the manacles, freeing Cassie's hands. It didn't do her any good. Straight away Richard and another of the Few took a wrist each, holding her as tightly as any chain, their fingers like steel.

'Please,' said Richard nervously. 'Try to relax.'

Oh, *sure*.

Someone was loosening the chains on her feet, though

they weren't removed altogether. As soon as the tension was released, Richard and his colleague tugged her so that her head tipped off the end of the stone table, and her shoulders rested on the edge. Her neck hurt crazily now, but she could at last see the presence behind her, even if it was upside down. A thin, stooped figure, crooked with age. Upswept white hair, fragile porcelain skin, and a kind smile distorted by the angle.

Madame Azzedine.

The old woman sat in a gilded chair, her face close to Cassie's. Her frail hands slipped under Cassie's head to support it, easing the ache in her neck. Cassie stared up into the blue crinkled eyes, only inches away. The old woman seemed almost overcome with joy.

'Thank you for this, Cassandra, my dear.' Dry wrinkled thumbs stroked her temples. 'I liked you the moment I met you, do you know that?'

'No! What are you—'

'Look at me, Cassandra. I'm old. I've had all from this body I could possibly have expected. It's time for Madame Azzedine to . . . bow out. It's time for me to take a new body. A young body.'

She smiled down lovingly at Cassie. 'Your body.'

Frozen with terror, Cassie searched the woman's face. Something moved behind those pale old eyes, and she

226

couldn't think why she hadn't seen it before. Maybe she had. Something swirling, roiling. Whose eyes had done that too: boiled with life and an animal glow? Didn't matter. Somehow she knew what was coming now. No way to stop it: only delay it. Talk. *Talk*.

'What are you going to do when you're finished with me?' She breathed hard, smothering her fear with anger. 'Shuck me off like an old snakeskin? Just like with Madame Azzedine?'

'Come, come –' she laughed that tinkling laugh, 'I've had a long, good life. I've been strong, and powerful, and beautiful. You can expect the same! You have nothing to lose, Cassandra. Nothing.'

'Except my soul!' yelled Cassie. 'Right? Except my*self*.'

She could no longer see any face but Madame Azzedine's.

'Now, Cassie. Do you think your friend Richard has lost himself? Ranjit, Ayeesha, Katerina? Do you think Sir Alric has lost himself?' A girlish giggle. 'Certainly not. We are still ourselves. We have given the spirits corporeal presence, that's all. They have not overwhelmed us. They have *joined* us.'

'Spirits?' Cassie tried to breathe properly. Madame Azzedine's scent was overwhelming, and the stone was painfully hard against her back.

'Ancient spirits, so ancient,' mused the old woman. 'A new life with every generation. You cannot expect us to fade away and die for the convenience of a few mortals. Especially when those mortals have so much to gain.'

'Like what?' Terror was starting to choke her again. Who was talking to her? Madame Azzedine, or the thing inside her? Maybe even the old woman didn't know any more. The wrinkled lips were closer to Cassie's own now, the aged face dreamy.

'Everything, scholarship girl.' Katerina's cold tone was merciless. 'There is everything to gain! We hosts are not lost souls. The spirit merely adds its essence to our own.'

'Spirit? Is it a demon or what?'

'Don't be so rude.' The Swedish girl sounded more amused than Cassie would have thought possible. 'With the *spirit* we are stronger, crueller, more ruthless. More beautiful. Better equipped for today's world, in other words.'

'You're sick!'

'No. Personally, I've never felt better. What would you like to be, Cassie, when you grow up?' Katerina sniggered. 'A prime minister? A president? Head of an international corporation? An A-list celebrity? Some of us are, you know. Though for you, perhaps we should talk D-list.'

'*I want to be myself!*'

'But you will be,' soothed Madame Azzedine. 'That and more.'

'*No!*'

'Too late, my dear.'

Dry lips fastened over hers, powerful, irresistible. The smell of death and perfume swept over her so that she almost gagged, but it was impossible to make a sound, let alone vomit. Cassie squirmed, waiting to feel what Alice had felt, waiting for the life to be sucked out of her. Did it hurt? It had looked as if it did. A tear trickled to her hairline. She tried one last time to struggle, but the grip on her wrists was too strong. From the circle of the Few came a low howl of collective excitement.

Then the worst bolt of pain yet shot through her head, her heart leaped in her chest like an animal trying to escape, and the whole world went blinding white.

And somebody, somewhere, screamed.

CHAPTER TWENTY

It wasn't weakness. It was *strength*.

Cassie was suddenly alert, completely alive. Madame Azzedine's scrawny neck was so close she couldn't focus properly, but she could see purple veins bulging and throbbing, could feel the old body beginning to jerk and tremble, could taste rotten flesh. Their mouths were still locked together but she no longer felt sick.

She felt *strong*.

The distant shriek came again, and Madame Azzedine released Cassie's head abruptly, clenching her fists until the knuckles showed bone-white through thin skin. Cassie expected her head to smack down into the stone table, but it didn't. There was power in her neck; it didn't even hurt to keep her head up. Nor did she lose contact, even as the ancient body squirmed and the woman tried to twist away.

Another agonised wail, as if it came from very far away, and Cassie knew that Madame Azzedine wasn't making this racket out loud, only inside Cassie's head. The grip on her arms loosened a little, and Cassie strained hungrily upwards. For an instant, Madame Azzedine broke the contact, and Cassie had a glimpse of her white, tortured face. Katerina snapped out a word, and her arms were released.

Cassie lunged up and grabbed Madame Azzedine's head. Yanking the old mouth back down to her own, she twisted her fingers into the white hair.

She needed it. It needed her. No problem . . .

Something was burning her shoulder blade, a concentrated, intense pain, but she didn't mind. What she had to do was keep contact. Keep the old woman close. Nothing else mattered. Hot needles in her shoulder. No, no. Didn't matter . . .

Another scream. Not in her head, though. It was real and close, and it seemed terribly familiar. Irate. Tempestuous. Drama-queeny.

Latin American . . .

Something hard whacked into the side of Madame Azzedine's skull, snapping it away. Cassie grabbed at the old woman as she slumped silently to the side, but with her own legs still restrained she couldn't catch her. As the body crumpled to the floor in a dry, dead heap, a twist of translucent white drifted from the old woman's lips, spiralling towards the ceiling with a high, squealing wail.

Katerina snatched at the escaping wisp. 'Fools!' she howled. 'What have you done?'

Cassie's sentiments exactly. Her fingers clawed at the fleeing mist as well, until with a cry of frustration she curled up, tearing at the chains. Then she froze, breath caught in her throat.

There he was.

Ranjit stood in front of her, cold and still, facing the rest of the Few. His back was to her but she clearly heard his grim murmur. 'You bitch, Katerina. What have you done?'

Katerina hunched, spitting with rage, but didn't reply.

So Ranjit wasn't in on this *unofficial* ceremony? As if Cassie's head wasn't spinning fast enough already . . . Did this mean he was on her side?

In which case, what the hell had kept him?

To her left, Cassie caught a glimpse of Jake slashing Keiko's weird knife in a broad warning arc at the snarling Few. Isabella had clambered on to the stone table and now stood above Cassie, threatening all comers with what looked like a very long, very whippy hammer.

'Where did you get that?' shouted Cassie, rubbing

her temples fiercely, fighting to focus.

'This?' Isabella swung at a hooded figure as it made a lunge for her, cracking her weapon into its head. The figure dropped like a stone. 'I bring this to school every term, Cassie! I knew it would come in handsome.'

'Handy,' said Cassie, shaking her head clear at last.

'I told you,' Jake called over his shoulder, his focus still on the semicircle of malicious Few, who eyed his knife with extreme wariness.

'Yeah, yeah,' said Cassie. 'I know. Killer with a polo mallet.' Wrapping one ankle chain round her fist, she strained at it, but it was hopeless.

Ranjit's voice was low but clear. 'Jake. The chains. Use the knife.'

Jake threw him a mistrustful scowl. 'Like that's going to—'

'I said, use the knife!'

With a last suspicious glower, Jake backed up, then turned and slammed the knife down on to the chain. The links shattered, but he had already turned to warn off two more of the Few, who had sprung forward to within striking distance. They hesitated, snarled, retreated one step. Then another.

Jake glanced down at the knife in shock. 'That's some blade.'

Ranjit took no notice. He stood perfectly still, and none of the Few dared to approach him. His focus was all on Katerina, something crackling between them. Lust? Fury? Hatred?

Oh, who the hell cared.

'Jake!' yelled Cassie, tightening the other chain. 'Again, quick!'

One more swift strike, and stone chips erupted in a puff of dust from the table. Jake swore.

'Missed. Do it again!' screamed Cassie.

Once more, and three links on the second chain disintegrated. *Right*. Cassie jumped down from the table in time to punch one of the hooded figures hard as it finally leaped at Jake. Cassie's fist connected with what must have been a jaw, making a satisfying noise, and the attacker reeled back.

'Nice timing,' said Jake, who looked embarrassed about ducking.

'You too. How'd you get here?'

Isabella was whirling the polo mallet above her head. 'Tell you later. Can we *go now*?'

'Yeah. *Back off!*' Jake yelled, as a figure slunk out of the shadows on his left. Katerina was pale and immobile with fury.

'*You* have the blade!' she hissed. '*You*.'

'I'm really sorry,' said Jake. 'Is that against school rules?'

'Don't do the banter thing,' moaned Isabella. 'Let's *run*. Cassie. Go!'

Cassie shoved forward between Isabella and yet another hoodie, who was stalking murderously towards the Argentinian. Drawing back her lips, Cassie growled. Funny how naturally that came . . .

Ranjit and Katerina were still all wrapped up in each other, as if they were fighting some sort of psychic duel. He obviously wasn't concerned with the other Few. He was as motionless and menacing as stone, but his eyes blazed.

This could get bad, Cassie knew it in her bones. 'Isabella! Jake! Back to the door, come on!'

But Isabella was hesitant now. 'Ranjit's in trouble.'

'He can look after himself,' yelled Jake. 'Go, Isabella!'

But Cassie hung back too. Ranjit still stood deathly quiet, facing down the Few, but now they were regaining their courage, circling him. Cassie started towards him, despite Isabella dragging on her arm.

'Cassie, come on! Please!'

Richard stood at the far side of the table, sorrow and disappointment in his beautiful eyes. Cassie hesitated, read on his lips the word, *Please* . . . She didn't answer as they slipped into the archway beneath the writhing snakes. A stone tongue flickered out, almost touching her shoulder, and she winced.

'Cassie!' shouted Richard again. 'Please!'

Her lip curled. 'Go play with the traffic, Richard.'

She shoved Jake. 'Get out of here!'

Isabella was holding him back. 'What about Ran—'

'Come *on*,' shouted Jake. This time he pulled Isabella with him.

Cassie lingered. Katerina was snarling orders at the hesitant Few as they surrounded Ranjit.

'Leave, Cassandra,' he said, cold as marble. 'I'll follow.'

Stupid to argue. Stupid, too, to feel this terrible fear for him. He knew what he was doing. Didn't he? Reluctantly, she turned on her heel, and ran after Jake.

Jake and Isabella were both fast runners, but she caught up with them easily. 'How did you find me?'

'When you didn't come back to the room at the time we agreed, we went looking for you,' explained Isabella breathlessly. 'We looked all over the Academy. Eventually, we went to the Few's common room.'

'Obviously you weren't there,' Jake added, 'but neither were half of the Few. Ayeesha was, and Cormac, and a couple more, but they said that Katerina and the others had gone to meet Richard. That's when we knew you were in trouble.'

'And then Ranjit came in,' said Isabella.

'Yeah. And he knew where they'd take you,' spat Jake. 'Funnily enough.'

The passageway seemed terribly long and winding, snaking uphill at an increasing gradient, but Cassie ran effortlessly; she must be fitter than she thought.

'Jake, that is unfair!' protested Isabella breathlessly. 'Ranjit did not know about the – the ceremony!'

'He says,' muttered Jake grudgingly.

'He only guessed what had happened, Jake! And he brought us to the Arc, didn't he? Showed us the secret door?' Panting, she threw Cassie a wicked grin. 'So he does have the hots for you! See?'

Turning once again to focus on the way ahead, Isabella gave a shocked gasp. As she skidded to a halt, Jake almost fell over her.

'What the *hell*—'

'Hello, Jake, sweetie.'

Ahead of them, blocking their way to the door, stood a slender figure, long pale hair gleaming. Katerina was smiling at them.

Sort of.

'Jeez,' muttered Cassie, 'that girl really is all teeth.' And such long, sharp ones too.

'You ought to know what you're truly up against,'

Katerina murmured throatily. *Very* throatily.

The girl didn't look herself any more, to put it mildly. The eyes were red, the skin grey, the lips pulled back in a rictus grin. And yet somehow it was still Katerina. Through and through.

'I should've known!' exploded Jake. 'It's a trap! Singh brought us here and now he's sent her after us.'

'No,' said Cassie flatly. 'Where's Ranjit, Katerina?'

With a trilling laugh, Katerina used a claw-hand to tuck a strand of hair behind her ear. 'She's right, Jake. I don't need *Ranjit's* help. You think I don't know these ancient labyrinths? I know them all, in every city. I've known them for centuries.'

'And you're looking your age,' said Cassie.

Katerina hissed. 'You are a pair of fools. She won't thank you, you know,' she told Jake and Isabella, jerking her head in Cassie's direction. 'In the end she won't. In fact she'll want you dead for that stupid interruption.'

Jake set his teeth. 'Get out of our way, Katerina. I don't want to hurt you.'

'No, seriously. You think I take orders from Scholarships?' A long tongue flickered out to lick Katerina's teeth as the horrible peeled-back grin returned. 'You think you *can* hurt me? You don't know me very well, do you? *Scooby.*'

Jake's intake of breath was high-pitched. '*What did you say?*'

'You heard. Scooby-dooby-doo. I can't tell you how loud she screamed for you, at the end. Didn't she ever use your real name?'

Jake seemed paralysed, though he was shaking. The knife hung limp and useless in his hand; any moment now it was going to slip from his fingers.

'You,' he said, barely audible. 'It was you?'

The vicious mouth twisted in a sneer. 'Oh, do grow up, Scooby. Of course it was me. Well, Keiko and me. Ranjit simply delivered her, that's all.'

Anxiously Cassie glanced at Jake. She couldn't even see him breathing, but she thought she could hear the hard thump of his heart.

'There was only a year between you two meddling kids, wasn't there? How close you must have been, you and Jess.'

'Yes,' whispered Jake.

'And you will be again. Let's finish this quickly.' Frowning, Katerina examined a nail like a yellow talon, dull and gnarled. 'I need to go and see my roommate.'

'Oh?' Isabella simmered with fury. 'Hungry?'

'Frankly, yes. Ingrid is delicious, and cooperative. Unlike Jessica. I'm sorry to say it, Jake, but your sister was

239

a little sour, a little bitter. All that running, you see, all that fear. All that adrenal—'

Jake roared and leaped at Katerina, slashing wildly with the knife. She dodged like a snake, escaping his grip and wrapping a powerful arm around his throat. Isabella went for her, screaming, but Katerina twisted Jake's neck back and ducked the swing of the polo mallet. Rebalancing, she kicked out hard, catching Isabella in the stomach and knocking her stunned and winded to the floor.

Cassie's blood felt so cold in her veins she couldn't move. Katerina's claws were digging into Jake's neck and he tore desperately at her arm, dropping the knife. Instantly, Cassie knew it was what she'd been waiting for. She dived for the knife, snatched a hank of Katerina's hair with the other hand and, as the Swede squealed with pain, she swung the blade wildly across Katerina's cheek. Blood sprayed.

Oops, thought Cassie, still gripping the girl's monstrous head. What now . . . ?

After a second's horrible silence, Katerina howled. Her grip on Jake loosened enough to let him catch a lungful of air, but she didn't let him go.

'Amateur!' she screamed in Cassie's face. 'How *dare* you!'

Cassie wasn't expecting the force of Katerina's blow. It knocked her to the far side of the passageway, and as she crashed against the wall the knife fell from her fingers and spun across the floor. Katerina lunged for it, her fingers closing on the writhing handle while the other claw-hand kept a grip on Jake's throat. Cassie tried to scramble to her feet but her head was spinning crazily again. A few feet away, Isabella was still trying to suck breath into her lungs. The blade of the knife shone as Katerina raised it.

'Now watch Jake die,' she smiled.

But something moved faster than the blade, slamming hard into Katerina, knocking her sprawling. Dropping both Jake and the knife, wailing with rage and fear, Katerina kicked and fought uselessly against her new attacker. She looked, thought Cassie, like a leopard trying to fight off a tiger. When the two writhing, struggling bodies tumbled against the passage wall, Cassie saw the tiger clearly. Ranjit.

His teeth were viciously bared, and his eyeballs, like Katerina's, were red from corner to corner. His powerful hands found her throat and Katerina squirmed, rasping for breath, lashing her claws across his face and drawing blood. But far more of it leaked from the knife-gash in her own cheek; Ranjit's hands were soaked in it. Finally wrenching his blood-slick fingers loose, Katerina screamed hoarsely and gave him a savage kick in the chest. He stumbled back, and she scrambled on to all fours, spitting.

'Get out of my sight, dark-sister,' growled Ranjit. 'Before I kill you.'

'Never,' hissed Katerina, one bloody hand clutching her cheek. 'Never. It's her I'll kill. Oh, you won't kill me.'

She stared at him greedily for a moment. Then she leaped to her feet, and ran.

For what seemed an age, the four of them stood in silence. Jake was the first to move, lifting Isabella to her feet. Cassie was not at all sure her roommate needed to press so close against Jake, or hang quite so limply in his arms, but what the hell. Cassie managed a smile, but it died as Jake leaned down and fumbled once again for the knife. It trembled in his fingers as he pointed the tip of it at Ranjit. His mouth was twisted with rage.

'Katerina said you . . . said you *delivered* her. To be killed.'

Ranjit didn't blink. His eyes were normal again, if dull, and the skin of his face was pale and taut. 'She was lying. How could I hurt Jess? I loved her.'

'You didn't help Katerina?'

'No. I had arranged to meet Jess. But I was late, somebody delayed me. It was deliberate, I realised that afterwards, but I was too stupid to see it at the time. I swear, Johns— Jake. I didn't kill her, and I didn't take her to be killed.'

For the first time, Jake looked uncertain.

'So why was she?' he asked, and in the terrible silence added quietly, 'Killed.'

'Katerina.' Ranjit shrugged helplessly. 'I didn't know how much she . . . how much she—'

'Wanted Jess out of the way?' said Cassie, realisation dawning. 'So she could have you all to herself?'

He gave her a long, unhappy look. 'Yes.'

'And what about Keiko?'

Ranjit sighed. 'She used to be Jess's best friend, before she was chosen. But after she joined the Few, she changed. Became more reckless – dangerous, even. She was crazy enough to go along with Katerina just for the hell of it.'

Cassie didn't say anything. If she opened her mouth she'd say, And who delayed you, Ranjit? Who was it that held you back long enough for them to kill Jess?

But the truth was, she didn't want to know.

Ranjit lowered his head. 'But even though I didn't hurt Jess, it's my fault Katerina and Keiko knew where to find her, so it's my fault that she's dead. I'm sorry, Jake. So sorry.'

To Cassie's ears, he sounded more than sorry. He sounded heartbroken. No wonder the guy had been keeping the rest of the school at arm's length. It wasn't snobbery, it was pain. How could anyone cope with that sort of guilt?

Cassie reached out for the knife, sliding her hand gently over Jake's and squeezing it. 'Jake? I think he's telling the truth. Please?'

His fingers tightened, holding the knife rigid, then suddenly went limp, and Cassie eased the knife away. Turning to Ranjit, she held it out to him.

'No.' He took a step back, wary. 'It's Jake's now.'

Jake stood there stiffly, still angry and confused. But as Cassie watched, Isabella slipped her arms comfortingly round his waist. A moment later, he put his arms round her, too.

'Take it, Jake,' said Cassie. 'Please.'

He looked at the knife for what seemed like an age. But when his mind was made up, he reached out and gripped it, grim and certain.

'What about the others?' Cassie pointed back down the dark passageway.

'They won't follow yet. Not without Katerina. They were just supposed to keep me occupied while she got to you. We . . . argued.' Wincing, Ranjit touched a deep gouge on his forearm. 'But they saw my point of view in the end. Still, I suggest we go quickly.' He raised his head. 'If Jake will let me.'

Jake hesitated, tensing. Isabella squeezed his shoulders. 'He took us to Cassie,' she whispered. 'He helped us.'

The air in the passageway, cold as it was, seemed heavy and oppressive.

'Jake, do you believe me?' Ranjit asked. 'About Jess?'

'Why would I?'

Ranjit gave a tiny shrug. 'No reason. Except I'm telling you the truth.'

'Maybe,' said Jake.

'Will you trust me, then?' Ranjit sounded almost desperate.

Jake took Isabella's hand firmly in his, and turned towards the hidden door.

'No. But I'll pretend I do. For now.'

CHAPTER TWENTY-ONE

Stupid pyjamas. Shouldn't these be too small for her? They were baggy and misshapen and faded; she remembered them well. She tugged out the shapeless hem and scowled down at the Bratz pictures all over the fabric. Wasn't she too old for these?

The corridor was in darkness. But a shadow moved, thin and malevolent as a crow. A click-click of heels. Jilly Beaton, checking to see if the children were OK. Because if they were, something must be done . . .

She grinned.

No hurry. No fear. Cupping her hands against the landing window, Cassandra peered down into the scruffy yard. One of the bins was upended, rubbish disgorged over the cracked concrete. That must have been what had woken her. A scrawny fox rooted around in the debris, but as if feeling her gaze, it froze and stared back at her, one forepaw still raised.

She smiled at it. The fox turned back to the spilled bin, and she turned back to the stalking shadow. It had paused outside Lori's door, pressing an ear to the thin wood to drink in the girl's homesick sobs. How old was Lori? Eight. Same age Cassandra had been when Jilly started destroying her from the inside out.

Tutting silently, she shook her head and followed. How had the woman got this far? Right to the door of Lori's room? Oh, yes. Because she'd let her. Poor, poor Jilly. A rat in a trap, she was.

Now, what to do? A threat to go to the authorities? Phone Patrick and demand he listen? Or simply raise hell and the whole house?

Nah.

Jilly had placed a hand on Lori's door, had started to turn the handle, but she stopped at a sound. Turned. Stared.

Hello, Jilly.

The woman's smile of sadistic anticipation died, and she shrank away as Cassandra walked towards her. Cassandra was only ten years old but the woman was terrified of her! She laughed. If this was a memory there was something wrong with it — she'd never dared confront Jilly when she was ten. But who cared? This was delicious. The woman cowered, whimpering.

Pathetic. Just like that senator's wife, Flavia Augusta, the one who'd tried to poison her. Pathetic, like the greedy priest in Renaissance Turin, the one with the not-very-celibate appetites. Like the foppish Lord Acton when she'd caught him alone – Christmas, 1790, wasn't it? – slow and staggering with drink and lust. They'd all been terrified of her, in the end.

Quite right too.

On to this one, then. Cassandra hated her. She'd made Cassandra afraid, she'd made her hate herself. She'd tried to suck out Cassandra's soul, and that wouldn't do. It wouldn't do at all. Well, now it was the woman's turn to be afraid, and wasn't she just! That was an understatement. She looked as if she might soil herself.

A kiss then, dear Jilly! One little fond kiss! Just to show there's no hard feelings. Just to show how it feels, to be drained of one's self. One kiss . . .

She put a hand on either side of the woman's head. Bending down, she smiled right into her eyes and squeezed, crushing those tight, vicious lips into a parody of a pout. And through her distorted mouth, the woman began to scream.

Behind the door, undisturbed, Lori sobbed herself softly to sleep.

But Cassie jerked awake.

*

She hadn't screamed out loud; Isabella's reassuring snores went on without interruption. Willing her

248

heartbeat to slow down, Cassie rubbed the back of her neck. On her face she could feel a cold breath of December air: the window was open. A window on to Paris, not Cranlake Crescent. She wasn't a ten-year-old in Bratz pyjamas; these ones might be cheap but they were her size. And if there was anything lurking outside, it was no urban fox.

What a dream. What a nightmare.

Slipping out of bed, she padded to the window and leaned right out, gulping in cold air. It made her dizzy.

Careful. You might fall.

'Of course I won't fall!'

Stiffening, she stared out at the web of lights that was the city. That hadn't really been a murmuring voice in her ear. So why had she answered it?

'Estelle?' she whispered.

Nothing. She breathed deeply. This was stupid.

What's stupid about justice, my dear? You could have it, you know that.

'What?'

You know what's possible. You know what you want. You promised me you'd take what you want. You promised me.

Cassie recoiled, gripping the windowsill, staring fixedly into the night.

You let her get away with it, Cassandra. Didn't you?

'What was I supposed to do? What *could* I do? Nothing!'

Because you were scared. That's all. Let me in, Cassandra! Let me in and you'll never be scared again. Of anyone! Together, you and me! Let me in!

Silence, a long dragging silence. She was imagining the voice, Cassie decided. She was sleepwalking. That was all. Hallucinating.

One day we'll find her, Cassandra.

She put her hands over her ears. 'Go away!'

She'll be there for us. Easy meat. LET ME IN!

'NO!'

'Cassie?' Isabella's sleepy grunt made her jerk away from the window and turn. 'Cassie, what's wrong? Who are you talking to?'

'Nobody!' Cassie's voice shook. 'Sorry, Isabella, I was dreaming.'

'Beside the *window*?' Isabella sat up, sceptical.

'I was, um . . . getting some air. I started to doze off. Go back to sleep.'

'Are you OK?'

'Fine.' Cassie turned back to the night, and muttered, 'We're fine.'

She waited until Isabella's breathing deepened and a snore rattled out, then she tiptoed to the bathroom.

Tugging down her pyjama top, she peered at her shoulder blade in the mirror. The mark wasn't as clear and defined as Richard's, and it didn't burn fiercely like Keiko's had done as she died. It looked a little blurred, and there seemed to be lines missing, places where the pattern was broken. But it was there.

She wouldn't sleep now. Trying her hardest to be quiet, she eased open the wardrobe and pulled out the dress Isabella had insisted on buying for her. *For Heaven's sake, Cassie! Shut up and call it an early Christmas present!*

Versace: the one she couldn't pronounce. Cassie grinned. The fabric rustled as she laid it on her bed, and she paused, but Isabella didn't stir. She never did, thought Cassie fondly. Cassie hadn't had a single unbroken night's sleep since the events at the Arc two weeks earlier, but none of her night-time pacings had disturbed her roommate. The sign of an easy conscience, of course.

Cassie stroked the beautifully cut dress. It felt cool and rich and smooth: everything she wasn't. She couldn't think how she was going to carry it off, but maybe it was fabulous enough to eclipse her lack of confidence. Was the taffeta greenish-yellow or yellowish-green? She couldn't decide. Isabella said it matched her eyes.

Shame she didn't have a partner for the ball. She couldn't even *use* Richard, she thought guiltily. He'd been avoiding her like a virus. A contagious, fatal one. In fact he'd barely spoken to anyone since he'd been called to Sir Alric's office, the day after the ceremony at the Arc. God knew what Sir Alric had said to him, but it had left Richard silent and ashamed and, thought Cassie, a touch resentful. He wasn't himself.

Hah. *Not himself*: that was for sure.

Neither, of course, was she.

Richard had got off lightly, and so had the others, compared to their ringleader. From the tree-shaded colonnade, Cassie had watched Katerina's elegant exit from the Darke Academy, just twenty-four hours after she'd fled from them in monstrous form. The blonde beauty had sashayed down the steps, head high, hair and skin shining like any normal prom queen's. She'd worn big dark glasses, blood-red lipstick, and a brand new diagonal scar on her cheekbone. That, thought Cassie, had healed remarkably quickly, but it wasn't going to go away entirely. How did the immaculate Hitchcock blonde feel? she wondered. About scarring, disgrace, expulsion? Was she regretful? Not likely. Vengeful?

Sir Alric had stood at the top of the steps, watching Katerina until she slid gracefully into the black limousine and the chauffeur had closed the door. Then he'd turned, and his eye caught Cassie's, just for a moment.

She was sure he'd shivered.

For two weeks Cassie had waited in trepidation for her own summons to his office, but it had never come. Darke seemed to be avoiding her almost as keenly as Richard was. Not that either of them would be able to avoid her tonight. It was the Christmas Ball. And everyone, even if they no longer felt like it, was required to go.

Despite recent events, the whole school was buzzing with subdued excitement. She couldn't feel any of it. The preparations, the plans, the gossip and anticipation: none of them meant anything. The Darke Academy was finished for her. It was finished *with* her.

She wouldn't see its enigmatic founder again. He was going to leave Cassie to work this mess out for herself, that was clear. She was an embarrassment, a mistake, a nasty accident dumped on him by a few of his indisciplined favourites. Sir Alric Darke probably couldn't wait to see the back of her. Well, Cassie didn't care. She was anxious, frightened, confused, but she didn't *care*.

She'd learned a lot. She'd go back to her old life, and survive. She always had.

In the meantime, she might as well party.

*

School wallflower, Cassie thought ruefully. What a way to end her less-than-glittering career at the Darke Academy.

At least the atmosphere was a lot happier without Katerina and Keiko: the band was good, the mêlée of students was in end-of-term high spirits, and the teachers chatted among themselves, watching the dancers fondly. They avoided Cassie, though. Even Herr Stolz had treated her with nervous politeness for the last fortnight.

Jake was a fabulous dancer, and so was Isabella, and though they'd tried to include her, Cassie was glad they were so wrapped up in each other. She didn't feel like being sociable, and loitering beside Cassandra and Clytaemnestra suited her fine. There was no better company for her in this mood.

'Good evening, Cassie.'

She jumped but didn't turn round. The voice was unmistakable, after all: burnt honey mixed with gravel.

'Hello, Sir Alric.'

'You're not dancing?'

'No.' She paused, then thought: What the hell. 'Estelle doesn't feel like it.'

There was a long silence while they stood together in the shadows watching the band and the shrieking, laughing students. Alice was looking well, thought Cassie, if a bit wobbly and tearful after four glasses of champagne. Richard was nowhere in sight; he'd put in an appearance, then slunk away early. The rest of the Few seemed on top form. She'd been trying to picture each of them in a crimson hood, but it was no use.

'You don't know which of them were involved?' asked Sir Alric quietly.

Cassie shook her head. 'No. But it doesn't matter now.'

'It matters to me.'

'Well, then, you work it out. Thanks, by the way. I've had a great time.' She bit her lip. 'Mostly. Except for the bit with the chains and the demons.'

'Cassie . . .'

She waited for him to go on, and when he didn't, she turned her head to examine his face. It was very sober.

'You must come back next term,' he said.

'No, I don't think I must. Thanks all the same.'

'You don't understand.' He gave her an exasperated look.

'Tell me, then.' She cocked an eyebrow.

He sighed in defeat. 'The ritual may have been interrupted, but there's part of a spirit in you now. It wants to join with you fully. And it won't stop until it does.'

Cassie shrugged. 'Tough.'

'That's brave of you, my dear, but it isn't enough,' Sir Alric said with dark amusement. 'You either accommodate it, or defeat it. You can't run away from it.'

'I can try.'

'You'll never run fast enough for that, Cassie.' His tone was kinder than his words. 'Never.'

Uncomfortably she fiddled with her corsage. Isabella had chosen the stunning white orchid, plucked from the plant Jake had given her. She mustn't spoil it. She nibbled on a nail instead, then clasped her fingers.

'Go on,' she said at last.

'We're not all evil, Cassie. You've met the worst of us. You need to come back so that you can meet the best.'

Her lip curled. 'I don't want anything to do with any of you.'

'That's not an option, believe me. I'm sorry. I should have taken Estelle's little fantasies more seriously, but I never thought she'd have the nerve to defy me. It's a stubborn spirit you have inside you, Cassie. Stubborn and malevolent.'

'Half,' Cassie corrected him. '*Half* a stubborn, malevolent spirit.'

Sir Alric hesitated, took a deep breath. 'And one that still needs to be fed.'

With a small moan, Cassie put her face in her hands.

'You must have suspected it. Now do you see, Cassie? You have to return to the Darke Academy.'

She didn't speak, refused even to look at him.

'By the time you come back in the New Year, you'll be desperate to feed. The spirit will have begun to grow, to create the home it needs. That takes a lot of life force, Cassie, believe me.'

'So what if I starve it?' she growled.

'Believe me, Cassie, you'll feed.' He sounded sad. 'You don't know how, yet – not without causing harm. It's my job to teach you.'

'I'd never hurt anyone!' she said fiercely.

'But you will, when you grow hungry enough. When the spirit does, that is. You'll feed because you can't help yourself, and you could kill someone. Is that what you want?'

Slowly, Cassie shook her head.

'You'll feed. You'll have to feed your whole life; you'll feed on strangers, on people you know, on people you love.'

'No,' said Cassie desperately.

'Yes. Your spirit gives you beauty, strength and power. Do you think you get that for nothing?'

Now his voice held an aching melancholy, as if his head was bursting with memories. Cassie found she was trembling.

'It sucks the very life out of you, Cassie. That's why you have to suck it out of other people.'

'Oh.' Remembering Alice, she shut her eyes tight. 'Oh, God.'

'If you don't feed, the spirit inside you dies, and so do you. But it won't come to that. Before then, you will kill. You won't be able to stop yourself. I will teach you to feed without killing.'

'You'll teach me? So how are you going to do that? Lab rats? My friends?'

For the first time, he couldn't meet her gaze. His voice, when he spoke, was clipped and emotionless.

'That's the price our students pay, Cassie. It's the price they pay for being here.' His mouth twitched, humourlessly. 'For the . . . privilege.'

She couldn't repress a sound of revulsion as she backed away, but he gripped her arm suddenly, turned her to face him.

'So, Miss Bell. Will you die, or will you kill? Or will you do what's right, and come back?'

Cassie glared at him, determined to brazen it out, but his eyes terrified her. She thought she'd felt scared before: well, not like this. She nodded.

He breathed a satisfied sigh. 'Good. *Good*. I'm sorry it's necessary, Cassie, but it is.' His voice grew level again. 'Is there anything else I can tell you?'

Surveying the dance floor, touching Cassandra's cold

marble arm for comfort, Cassie nodded. But she waited till her voice was as cool as his.

'Where's Ranjit?'

EPILOGUE

The courtyard was in darkness, silent but for the faint rattle of talk and music and laughter, and the underlying throb of a bass beat, and, very distantly, the echo of the city. No night prowlers now. Jake was otherwise occupied.

Will you come back? she'd asked him.

I don't know. He'd chewed on a knuckle, avoiding her gaze. *It's unfinished business, Cassie. But what do I do?* At last he'd plucked up the nerve to look at her. *If the Darke Academy goes down, so do you. You're one of them now.*

Cassie shivered. But she trusted Jake. He wouldn't hurt *her* to find the truth, and real justice for Jess. They were friends. And Jake would come back to the Darke Academy. He must. *Unfinished business.* Besides, Isabella had wept bitter tears at the mere suggestion of Jake not returning. Cassie didn't know if she could handle her roommate's operatic heartbreak if the wretched boy didn't show up next term.

It wasn't as cold as it had been. Cassie counted the steps down to the courtyard: thirteen. Just as Estelle had said, on that very first day.

Funny, that. She wasn't thinking of her as Madame Azzedine any more.

A dark figure sat in moonlight at the edge of the pool. He didn't raise his head as she approached, but tore intently at something in his hand. As she drew closer, she saw shreds of velvety black drift into the still green water of the pool.

'Aren't those rare?'

Ranjit didn't smile. 'Very.'

She sat beside him on the curved stone rim of the pool. Leda's shadow spilled on to the flagstones, made monstrous by the swan on her neck.

At last he said, 'Your dress is beautiful. You look, um . . . beautiful.'

'Thanks.' She reddened, hoping he wouldn't see it, certain a blush would clash with the silk.

'What do you call that colour?'

'I dunno. Yellow? Pale green?'

He threw the last crumpled sliver of orchid into the pool. 'Chartreuse, I think.'

'Nice,' said Cassie. Trailing a finger in the cold water, weed drifting against her skin, she watched the moon's reflection shatter and re-form. 'What's going to happen to me?'

He opened his mouth, closed it again, then said, 'I don't know.'

'Oh, great. Neither does Sir Alric.'

He gave a low dry laugh. 'See, it's never been interrupted before. The ritual.'

She nodded, picked at trailing orchid roots. 'I'm different. I know that.'

'Uh-huh. Very.' Half-smiling, he pulled up another orchid, ripping its trailing root from the stone. 'They're not parasites, you know.'

'What?'

'Orchids. They're not parasites, they're epiphytes. They live on other living things, but they don't kill their host. The two, they . . . coexist.'

'That so?'

He laughed. 'Yes.'

'Are you in trouble, Ranjit?'

'That's the first time you've ever called me by my name, do you know that?' He shrugged. 'Some of the others . . . yes, they're angry. But what they did was wrong – helping Madame Azzedine, I mean. I don't have to be scared of them. Other way round, if anything.' His grin was one Cassie didn't entirely like. 'Well, they're not scared just of *me*, of course. They're afraid of what's inside me.'

She shuddered. 'And what is that, Ranjit?' Now she'd started using his name, it seemed difficult to stop.

'One of the worst of the dark spirits. The strongest, the oldest, the . . .'

'Baddest,' suggested Cassie.

'Uh-huh.' He smiled tightly. 'The baddest.'

'Now, you see,' she said, 'I'd have assumed that was Katerina's.'

'No. Me and my spirit? We have a personality clash.'

'Know what? I think I'm – *we're* – in the same boat.'

'Know what?' He laughed dryly. 'I think you might be right.'

Cassie submerged her fingers in the freezing water until they hurt. 'Katerina. Did she . . . Was she always like that? Or was she different? Before she was "chosen"?'

'Oh, she was always a *bit* like that.' He shrugged. 'Bad spirit, nasty person? It's not a good combination. Cormac, now: he has a good spirit, but you know what? He was always a bit of a rogue; and he still is. Ayeesha – good spirit, nice girl. You see? It's a synergy.'

'And you and me?'

'Two of the worst, Cassandra.' He seemed sad, but the

263

intensity of his look sent tremors down her spine that were not at all unpleasant. 'Two bad spirits, two OK people. At least, I don't think you're any worse a person than I am.' He gave her a skewed grin. 'I don't know what'll become of us. I suppose we'll find out.'

'Oh.' Leaning back, Cassie studied Leda, still reaching dreamily for the savage swan. 'Where will it be next term? The Academy, I mean. I assume you know?'

'Yes. We're going to be in New York.'

New York! She nodded, fighting a grin, struggling to show even a little reluctance. 'I won't miss that swan.'

'You won't have to. That comes with the Academy, wherever we go. All the statues do. And Sir Alric's little pets here.' Savagely, Ranjit tore another orchid from its anchorage. 'We're here for the convenience of the gods, Cassie. Or we're here to prey on mortals and take our fun. Gods and monsters. Depends which way you look at it.' He smiled without mirth. 'You see?'

'I see,' she said, and winked. 'I see both ways.'

He seemed bemused for a moment, but then he laughed.

'So,' said Cassie. 'About this *unacceptable* stuff.'

His questioning expression was nervous.

'Me. Remember? It wasn't that you didn't *like* me, but that you couldn't *accept* me.'

'Uh-huh . . .'

'So how's about it now, then?'

Ranjit rubbed his temples with his thumbs. *'How's about it?* What's that supposed to mean?'

'For someone with centuries of experience,' she murmured, 'you're not that bright, are you?'

As she pulled him towards her and kissed him, she thought: That's all boy, that is. Not spirit. *And I like him . . .* Yup. Part of Ranjit might be hundreds of years old, but what was a little age gap? This was fine. He wasn't sucking anything out of her; her heart was racing, but so was his. Her breath was high in her chest, but she could hear his, too: a little fast, a little yearning. And they both tasted kind of the same.

Of course you like him! So do I, my dear!

'*Estelle!*' Cassie shoved Ranjit's chest, propelling herself away. 'Go to hell!'

'Cassandra?'

'It's OK. It's OK.' She pulled him back for another kiss. 'It's just, there were three of us there, for a moment.'

They laughed, then Ranjit went quiet. 'You're coming back?' He gave her a nervous smile. 'Next year? You *are* coming back to the Academy, Cassandra?'

'Course.' Her quick smile faded. 'Jake too, I think.'

Ranjit grimaced. 'He wants to destroy me.'

'Yes. He thinks he's got reason.'

'What about you?'

'No.' Cassie shook her head firmly. 'I believe you. That's why I've got to come back. To stop him whupping your ass.' She returned Ranjit's grin, then shrugged. 'And of course, there's someone I have to deal with. Hear that, Estelle?'

Silence.

Ranjit curled his fingers round hers and squeezed hard. 'I wish you well, Cassandra. I wish I could fight mine. But we're one now. Joined for ever. How can you fight yourself?'

Cassie separated his fingers, thoughtfully, then brought his knuckles to her mouth and kissed them. Grinning, she unpinned her corsage, uncurled his hand and pressed the white orchid into his palm. 'Nothing ventured, gorgeous.'

This time he didn't smile back. 'You didn't know Estelle very well, did you?'

'Huh! I'm getting to know her better.' Cassie gave him another impudent wink. 'She likes you.'

'That's what I'm afraid of.'

He looked so sad and serious, Cassie grew instantly sober too. 'I don't want to know what she's like. Or what she's done or been.' She made a face. 'Do I?'

'Well not tonight, anyway.' He touched her lower lip with his thumb. 'I tell you what . . .'

'What?'

Up at the school's splendid entrance, light and music spilled over the top step. Ranjit pinned the white orchid back on to Cassie's bodice, then took her hand. 'I like it when you tell Estelle to go to hell. Tell her again for a couple of hours.'

'Just for a couple of hours?'

'Uh-huh. It's all you'll get, but it's long enough for a dance.' Cheerfully, he pulled her to her feet. 'You know this one?'

'Nah,' said Cassie. 'But I'll learn. That's why I came to a posh school, you know.'

Just for tonight, she thought, burying her face in his shirt to inhale his oh-so-human smell. This was fine, this was good. Just for tonight they were a boy and a girl, and they were nothing and nobody else, and they were dancing under a starry Parisian sky. Devil take tomorrow.

Though she hoped it wouldn't get the chance.

Turn the page to read an exclusive extract from the second book in the Darke Academy series: Blood Ties, *publishing early 2010.*

BLOOD TIES

'Hey, kiddo. Are we keeping you up?'

The voice sounded familiar, but somehow muffled and distant. As if it was coming from the bottom of a well. With an effort, Cassie Bell forced her eyes open and blinked woozily at the sight before her. The table was set with thirteen places. At the centre sat a pasty-looking turkey, clearly only big enough for eight. Cheap supermarket own-brand crackers and a paper tablecloth. Fatty chipolatas and overdone sprouts.

Christmas, Cranlake Crescent-style.

Could it really be only three weeks since she was eating exquisite French cuisine from fine china and crystal in the elegant dining room of the Darke Academy? It seemed a lifetime away.

'What's the matter?'

Cassie refocused on the sandy-haired figure across the

table. Oh, yeah, Patrick. Her key worker. The only thing that had made coming back to her old care home bearable. She managed a smile.

'Aren't you hungry, Cassie?' piped up Jilly Beaton sweetly from the head of the table. 'That's not like you. You've been eating us out of house and home for a fortnight.'

Cassie dug her nails into her palms. Jilly's bitchy remarks had been increasing ever since she had got back from Paris. Normally, Cassie wouldn't have given her the satisfaction, but her fuse seemed to be getting shorter every day.

'Yeah, well I just lost my appetite,' she snapped, pushing her chair back and getting to her feet. 'Excuse me.'

'Cassie Bell, you're not excused—' began Jilly, but Cassie was already out of the room.

Patrick caught her at the foot of the stairs, his face full of concern. 'Cassie, what's up? You've been acting funny ever since you got back from Paris.'

Cassie paused for a moment. What was there to say? Could she tell him the truth about the Academy? About the Few and their dark secret? About what had happened to her in that black place beneath the Arc de Triomphe? About their interrupted ritual that had left the spirit of Estelle Azzedine stranded, half-lodged in Cassie's mind?

About the strange hunger that had been growing inside her ever since, and how she knew that turkey and chipolatas just weren't going to hit the spot?

Impossible.

'I'm just missing my friends,' she mumbled. 'Y'know?'

An expression of relief washed over Patrick's face. 'Of course you are. Have you spoken to anyone today?'

'I had an email from Isabella last night. And one from, um, Ranjit.'

'Who's Ranjit?'

'Just a boy in one of my classes,' replied Cassie, flustered. 'Why?'

Patrick's grin grew wider and his blue eyes glittered. 'Because you blushed when you said his name.'

'Oh, give over!' Cassie gave him a playful shove.

'He's not your boyfriend, then?'

'No, he's not,' she said hurriedly.

'Uh-*huh*.'

'No. Really.' Cassie twisted her fingers into the cashmere sweater that her friend Isabella had sent her for Christmas. 'It's . . . complicated.'

Ha! That was the understatement of the century. Her few snatched moments with Ranjit at the end of term had hardly given them time to define their relationship. All she knew was that her stomach twisted with longing every time he came into her mind, but that he was back home in India. Thousands of miles away. She'd just have to put up with missing him – missing him like she could die of it.

Absorbed in her memories, she jumped at the sound of her ringtone. Pulling her phone from her jeans pocket, Cassie almost dropped it when she saw the name on the display. She felt the blood rushing to her face again.

'Speak of the devil,' chuckled Patrick as he went back into the dining room.

Cassie winced inwardly at his choice of words. She still didn't understand what the Few truly were. Gods and monsters, Ranjit had once joked bitterly. So which was he? Cassie didn't know. She wasn't sure that he knew himself.

Pushing her worries out of her mind, she clasped the phone to her ear like a lifeline. 'Ranjit!'

He must be able to hear the stupid grin she was wearing, even half a world away.

'Cassandra.' The soft warmth of his voice made her forget the freezing sleet and even, for a moment, the raging hunger. 'Happy Christmas.'

'Same to you.' Breathless, she sat down on the stairs. It was criminal how much she missed him. Criminal, and deeply inconvenient. 'Oh, it's good to hear from you.'

'Are you OK?' He sounded concerned.

'I'm fine. Fine. Just a bit . . .'

'The hunger is growing, isn't it?'

Cassie was quiet for a moment. It was a relief to speak to someone who knew what she was going through. Ranjit had been there before.

'Yes,' she said at last, and laughed shakily. 'You got it.'

'It won't be long, Cassandra. A week and a half. Will you be all right?'

'I'm fine. Honestly. I just . . .' She hesitated, then thought, Take a leap of faith, girl. 'I miss you. A lot.'

'Oh God, me too.' The vehemence in his voice was shocking, coming from the normally cool and collected Ranjit Singh. He almost sounded relieved. 'I miss you and I'm *worried* about you. Have you, ah, heard from Estelle?'

She swallowed. 'Once or twice. But the old bat's been quiet lately. I hope she's curled up and died of hunger.'

'It isn't going to happen, Cassie.'

'Yeah, I know.'

'Take care of yourself. Please?'

She smiled, couldn't help it. 'Course I will. And I'll see you soon.'

'Can't be soon enough.' He gave a low laugh. 'Listen, I have to go. I'll talk to you again when I can.'

Tears stung her eyes as her stomach twisted again. 'Bye, Ranjit. Happy Christmas.'

'And you, again. I miss you, remember.'

Cassie snapped the phone shut before she started to blub. She buried her face in her hands, shocked by the strength of longing. Oh, this was ridiculous. She was supposed to be *tough*. She'd get through this. The hunger to feed, the hunger for Ranjit . . .

Stop. *Stop*.

The trouble was, she *was* hungry. Overcome with a desperate, intangible hunger for something beyond mere food. But there was nothing she could do except wait it out. If you stayed off chocolate long enough, you lost the taste for it. If you lasted a few weeks without cigarettes, you wouldn't want them any more.

Yes, and if you give up breathing for a while, you'll lose the taste for oxygen!

Cassie stiffened.

Well, really, my dear. You do amuse me!

Ignore her, Cassie told herself. Don't pay any attention.

Easier said than done. Just the sound of Estelle's voice in her head was enough to send the hunger sweeping through her with renewed force, so that she almost lost her balance, tipping forward.

She heard a door open and close. Footsteps. A voice . . .

'Cassie? Are you OK?' Patrick's tone was concerned.

She leaped to her feet, fists clenched. *OK*? What did that mean? Of course she was *OK*! She'd never be less than OK, never less than powerful and beautiful and confident. The stupidity of the man!

No! He'd done so much for her. She didn't know what she'd have done without him.

Estelle's whisper was like the caress of a serpent. *And he could do so much more, my dear*.

Patrick looked nervous under her steady, feverish stare. Yes. Estelle was right. A good friend like Patrick would always give of himself. She could rely on Patrick. He was strong, young, confident. Perfect.

'Cassie?'

Ah, she was just so damn *hungry*. She stretched her lips into a rictus smile. 'I'm fine.'

Don't talk. Let him come closer. I can smell him . . .

Patrick took a pace back, and she thought she saw him shiver. 'Stop fooling around, Cassie. Your dinner's getting cold.'

You seem warm enough to me.

'OK, I'm sorry. I'll leave you in peace.' He was turning away. 'Come back when you're ready.'

'*STOP!*'

She launched herself from the step, almost flew

after him. Seizing his collar, she yanked him back, spinning him around. Her fingers found his jaw, gripping him, tugging him towards her. He tried to pull away, but he didn't stand a chance. Not a chance. She laughed out loud.

His eyes were full of terror, and his panicked breath was in her face. She could smell him again: oh, the *life* of him! Her lips were pulled back when she caught sight of a figure beyond the glass panel of the front door. For an instant her heart seemed to stop, and she stiffened and growled. A face snarled back at her, feral and mad, like a rabid animal. And then, with a sickening jolt to her gut, she knew. It wasn't some monster trying to break into the house. It was her own reflection.

'Oh, my God!' She let go of Patrick so fast he crumpled to the floor. She stumbled back and away from him.

His terrified eyes were locked on her, the bright blue dilated almost to black. She expected that. But she didn't expect the words that fell from his mouth.

'Oh God, Cassie. Not you. Not you!'

What?

For half a second she stood, hands over her mouth, staring at Patrick. Then she turned on her heel and fled. She didn't slow down as she took the stairs two at a time, crashed into her room, furiously grabbed a chair and jammed it under the handle. There. That was as safe as it got. As *he* got.

Cassie slumped to the floor, exhausted. It could have been worse, she told herself, as her heartbeat slowed. So much worse.

Ah, who was she trying to kid? She'd lost control. She could have hurt Patrick. Killed him even. Jamming her fists into her mouth, Cassie bit down until she drew blood. A few more days, that was all. A few days and she'd be back at the Academy. Back with its mysterious principal Sir Alric Darke. He must be able to help her fight this. She'd see no one until then.

But Cassandra, my sweet, I'm HUNGRY!

The plaintive, angry voice echoed and bounced around her skull, it felt so light and empty. She was dizzy with hunger. But she'd control it. It was just a few days. Only a matter of time . . .

That's right! In the echo-chamber of her head, Estelle sounded vindictive and ravenous, but triumphant. *Oh yes, Cassandra, my dearest girl! Only a matter of time . . .*

the Vampire Diaries

itv 2 Now a major itv2 series

www.bookswithbite.co.uk

Sign up to the mailing list to find out about the latest releases from L. J. Smith

DARK HEART FOREVER

When Jane Jonas develops a friendship with an enigmatic stranger in town, it's exciting, it's new, and Jane wants him more than she's ever wanted anybody – until her mystery dream boy gets in the way.

Now Jane is caught between two worlds: one familiar, but tinged with romance and excitement; the other dark and dangerous, where angels, werewolves, and an irresistible stranger are trying to seduce her …

www.bookswithbite.co.uk

Sign up to the mailing list to find out about the latest releases from Lee Monroe